THE
RAIN
HERON.

Robbie Arnott

atlantic·*fiction*

First published in Australia in 2020 by The Text Publishing Company.

Published in hardback in Great Britain in 2020 by Atlantic Books, an imprint of Atlantic Books Ltd.

This paperback edition published in Great Britain in 2021 by Atlantic Books.

10 9 8 7 6 5 4 3 2 1

A CIP catalogue record for this book is available from the British Library.

Paperback ISBN: 978 1 83895 128 3
E-book ISBN: 978 1 83895 127 6

Printed in Great Britain

Atlantic Books
An imprint of Atlantic Books Ltd
Ormond House
26–27 Boswell Street
London
WC1N 3JZ

www.atlantic-books.co.uk

For the McKenzies

THE
RAIN
HERON

PART 0

A FARMER LIVED, but not well. If she planted grain, it would not sprout. If she grew rice, it would rot. If she tried to raise livestock, they would gasp and choke and die before they'd seen a second dawn (or they were stillborn, often taking their mothers, which the farmer had usually bought with the last of her coins and hope, with them). Success and happiness were foreign to her, and she had forgotten what it was like to go to bed unhungry. All she had was her hunger and her farm—and her farm, as far as she could tell, wanted her to starve.

Her struggles weren't due to laziness or a lack of skill. She had been raised on farms, her parents and grandparents had been farmers, and she knew as much about crops and soil and animal husbandry as anyone else in the valley where she lived. She worked hard and long, under a harsh sun and in bone-soaking rain. When she'd exhausted every technique she'd learned from her family, she turned to books, experiments, strange fertilisers, none of which helped. No enemy had salted her fields or cursed her name, for she had no enemies—she was liked and respected by all the people of the valley. There was no reason for her farm's failure. Yet her crops continued to rot, and her livestock continued to die.

Six years after her parents died and left her on the farm alone—six years of hungry, dismal failure—a black storm blew over the mountains and into the valley. Thunder crashed through walls; lightning licked trees; the wind grew fangs and chewed barns into splinters. Worst of all was the rain. Oceans of freezing, sideways-blown water heaved onto the farms of the valley, turning paddocks into lakes and ponds into seas. These wide waters soon swelled the river that ran through the valley, hastening its current, carrying away topsoil, crops, herds, fences and outbuildings. People took shelter in their stone houses as animals died outside in the chocolate flood. Behind their old, thick walls, they were safe. Everyone was accounted for—everyone but the unlucky farmer.

After the storm stopped raging it took a full day before the floodwaters began to drop. Only then could the people of the valley venture out, in fishing boats and on upturned dining tables, to try to salvage their property. It was at the dusk of this day—a day of sorrowful searching, of fishing with colanders and paddling with hatstands—that they found her. As the weak sun dipped, a group of teenagers, piloting an ancient coracle, saw something strange in the limbs of an old, leafless oak. Paddling nearer, they saw that it was the unlucky farmer, dead or unconscious, her body draped over the branches like a nightgown hung out to dry. But more curious than this was what they saw next: a huge heron, the colour of rain, suddenly emerging from the flood in a fast, steep flight, leaving not even a ripple on the water beneath it. With a languid flap of its wings it came to rest in the crown of the oak, standing over the unlucky farmer, as if on guard.

The teenagers brought their boat to a stop. This water-risen heron was unlike any other they'd seen before—any other heron, any other living creature. Its blue-grey feathers were so pale, they claimed later, that they could see straight through the bird. Its body was pierced by strands of dusky light, and the tree was clearly visible directly behind its sharp, moist beak.

A ghost, one claimed. A mirage, said another. But before they could get closer the heron hunched its neck, flapped its wings and leapt into the sky. A thick spray of water fell from its wings, far more water than could have been resting on its feathers. Then it disappeared into the remnants of the storm.

The teenagers watched it vanish, not sure what they were seeing, not trusting their tired eyes and waterlogged minds. At that moment the unlucky farmer rolled in her cradle of branches, coughed out a spurt of black mud and sucked at the air with great need, great violence.

THE FLOODS RECEDED. Fences were mended, barns rebuilt, crops resown. Within a few months the valley's farms were back to normal. All except for the fields of the unlucky farmer.

Where once her wheat had refused to sprout, it now blanketed the fields in shining rows of blond. Where her rice had rotted, it now surged forth from the water, pearly, fat and firm. And where her animals had died, they now grew and frolicked—goats, cattle, geese, chickens, every creature under her care. The success of her farm came fast and hard, and soon she was hiring labourers to build fences, harvest grain, herd flocks, which helped the farm flourish yet more. Her prosperity grew; her troubles became memories; a warm pulse began throbbing in her stomach.

On cloudless nights the great heron could be seen flying above her fields, cold rain spraying from its wings, the moon shining clear and bright through its feathers.

Over the seasons her farm continued to thrive, becoming the most successful in the valley. She built herself a large stone house, but that was the only concession she made to her newfound wealth. The rest of her money she shared among the community. The lessons she'd learned while poor—lessons of respect, of kindness, of compassion—she refused to abandon. She helped pay for roads, bridges, a school. Hunters were given free use of her land, fishermen free range of her creeks. Travellers came to know that they were always welcome in her house, that they were sure to find a warm fire and a dry bed waiting for them. She sponsored bright students; she paid for doctors to visit the valley; she hosted grand feasts at the end of every harvest.

Still the heron soared overhead.

Her neighbours were pleased for her, happy that her years of struggle had been rewarded with good fortune. They weren't surprised that she was sharing her riches. She had been a good person while poor; why wouldn't she be a good person now? All were happy; all were content. All but the son of her closest neighbour.

PERHAPS IF HE had been older, he wouldn't have done it. With more winters in his bones he may have been kinder, less jealous, more contemplative. Or maybe not—inside this boy there was a bitter kink, and perhaps no amount of time or experience could have untwisted it.

Where the other valley folk saw well-deserved luck, the neighbour's son saw unfairness. He was too young to remember how desperate she had been; all he knew was that she prospered while he and his father grew hungry. He watched her fields teem with golden wheat as his father's, stripped of topsoil, lay fallow. He heard the music and laughter of her feasts at the same time as he heard the growling of his stomach. He saw her bridges gleam in the sun; he saw the clever students lugging books in and out of her school; he watched oxen drag ploughs through her fertile earth. And every evening, above all these sights and sounds, he saw the ghostly heron.

With each stroke of the bird's wings his vision of unfairness turned closer to envy. Envy grew to anger, and anger gave way to rage. One night he felt that he couldn't wake up another morning to see the shame on his father's face, the shame and the hunger and the sorrow and the misery, against the backdrop of their neighbour's wealth. In the darkest part of that night he thrashed in his sheets as his thoughts twisted in on themselves, losing logic, churning sick. None of it had happened before the heron appeared; if the heron went, so too would the injustice. When he heard his father's breathing steady into a familiar pattern he got up, found his pocketknife and left the house.

The night was cold and clear. He walked beneath a sky studded with stars. The wind pawed at his clothes as he reached the farm border, vaulted the fence and crossed their neighbour's fields. No dogs barked; no doors opened. He kept marching, the rattling chain of his thoughts just holding together, loose but strong, dragging him forward. Two fields he crossed, then three. A bridge. A creek. Another field, and he had reached his destination: the leafless oak that had saved his neighbour during the storm.

Other children had told him the heron roosted here—children who had been to his neighbour's feasts, who'd watched the bird settle into its branches. The tree was empty now, but the boy wasn't in a hurry. He waited. Hours passed. The wind rushed, raking ice across his cheeks. His legs cramped; his hands shook; his eyes streamed. Still he waited, until finally, in the hour before dawn, the bird shot out of a nearby stream and came to perch on a high branch of the tree. Water trickled from beneath its talons. The boy could see straight through its body, although the bright points of starlight in the sky were rendered watery and distorted. The rage he'd felt earlier came over him again, hot and foul, and he began creeping towards the tree. If the heron noticed him it made no sign, not even when the boy had scaled the lower branches and was closing in on its roost.

When he was within reach of the heron, the boy paused. The wind was as strong as ever, yet the bird's feathers weren't moving. He wondered at this for a moment, at wings that could use the air but not feel it; but again he felt the burn of his rage. He drew the knife, snapped open the blade. Rearing up, he balanced on the branch using his feet alone, and readied to grasp the heron's neck with his free hand while he cut its throat with the knife. Yet when he reached out to grab at the plumage, he felt no feathers—only a sensation of cold liquid, of wetness, of running ice. And with it came sudden feelings of guilt and sorrow, sensations that plunged from his fingers up his arm, through his veins, into his guts and lungs and heart. Only then, in the howling of the wind and the fullness of the night, did the heron turn its face to his.

THE FOLLOWING MORNING brought unseasonal heat. Harsh light blanched the fields of the valley and warm winds stripped moisture from the grass. The once-unlucky farmer found her neighbour's son wandering in one of her farthest fields. He was moaning, sounds of great pain and horror, and when she approached him she saw that his eyes had been torn out. Dark blood had flowed down his cheeks and neck, spreading in blooms across his shirt, blood that had dried and caked into flaky cherry masses, even as fresh blood continued to pulse from the empty caves in his face. Viscera, veins and cartilage winked out at her, grey-white-blue, from amid the redness in the sockets. He was limping, too; one of his ankles and both his wrists were injured, as if he had fallen from a great height.

She lifted the bleeding boy in her arms and ran him to her neighbour, shouting for help from her farmhands on the way. A doctor soon arrived to treat the boy. He would survive, this doctor later told the people gathered in her neighbour's house, and he was lucky to have been found. In this heat, with no sight, with so much blood lost, he would have collapsed and died within hours.

The boy never spoke of what had happened to him; if pressed, he would say that he couldn't remember, that he must have been sleepwalking. Not many people believed him, least of all his father, but as he recovered they relented, largely because they were consumed by a larger problem: the heat that had come the morning he'd been discovered, blind and bleeding, had not left. Instead it had grown hotter and stronger, pelting down endless rays of skin-burning, crop-roasting, pond-parching light. It was supposed to be mid-autumn—cool, rainy, gusty—yet the valley was a furnace. Dams emptied in weeks. Livestock thinned, panted, died. Irrigation ditches were dug, which only served to weaken the flow and depth of the river while the ditch-running water evaporated before it hit the fields. No farm was spared; nobody escaped the heatwave.

Worst hit of all was the once-unlucky farmer. She had the healthiest fields, so she lost the largest crop. She had the biggest herds, so she lost the most water to their endless thirsts and the most livestock to the drought that followed. After her crops and livestock she lost her farmhands, her wealth, her security. She should have seen it coming, some muttered. After all, they said, nobody had spotted the great heron since the first morning of the heatwave. They sympathised with her, but they all had losses and problems of their own, and they could not help her.

AFTER A FULL season of heat the twice-unlucky farmer woke one morning to see barren fields in every direction, scattered all over with dust and sun-bleached bones. The air shimmered as it rose from the dry ground, distorting everything she saw. She looked up to the wide pale sky and saw nothing but an endless dome of blue-yellow burn. She listened for the harsh cry of the heron and heard nothing but the drone of flies. She reached for a shovel, thinking she might dig a well, but its metal handle, heated by the sun, singed her palm. She threw it to the ground, clutching her hand.

The burn became infected. The valley's doctor had left weeks earlier, and a fever took hold first in her flesh, then in her mind. She wandered through her dead fields, raving incoherently, frothing at the mouth, pus oozing from her hand. Days later she was found by her neighbour, the father of the blind boy. He had seen her roaming and ranting from his window, and had thought to bring her a jug of water. He discovered her body, broken and still, at the base of the leafless oak.

PART 1

SOLDIERS HAVE COME to the village.

Ren looked up, avoiding Barlow's words, resting her eyes on the pines that crowded the sky, swamp-green, thick, heavy with resin that stuck to skin and cleared throats, nostrils, eyes.

Barlow was sitting on a large rock. When she didn't answer, he kept talking.

They're after something—they won't say what. But it's up here. On the mountain.

Ravens called from the trees, deep rasps, long and loud. Ren watched them hop, black patterns in the branches. Pine needles carpeted the ground beneath them, giving way in small glades to grass, stones, fallen branches, thick moss. The light was weak, interrupted everywhere by the trees and their shadows. Ren stretched her neck and stared at a pine cone.

It doesn't matter.

It does if they find you.

She walked to the rock he was sitting on and lay down what she was carrying: deerskins. Five, all small, but clean and neat and cured, free of blood and thick with fur that seemed to glisten in the green-dark light. In her swift movements, in the walking and laying down of the skins, she made it clear that the conversation was over, that she wouldn't be speaking any more about these soldiers.

Barlow did not like this, and with his long look of worry and the crossing of his arms he made sure she knew it; but, as with everything Ren did, he accepted it. He let his narrow, bearded face relax as he pushed himself off the rock and began inspecting the skins, running his fingers through the fur, murmuring about the quality, small imperfections, price, the coming winter.

Ren waited.

The ravens cawed on. The light weakened further. Finally, Barlow turned and offered two packets of vitamins, a handful of seeds, a woollen blanket and a pair of leather boots in exchange for the pelts. Ren nodded. Barlow undid the pack sitting beside the rock and dug out the goods.

Ren kicked off her old boots—worn, thin-soled, full of holes—and slid on the new ones. She threw the blanket over her shoulders, feeling its itch, its warmth, and put the vitamin packets and seeds in her pockets. She wriggled her torso, shifting the weight of the blanket.

More of the same next time?

He nodded. Any skins are good. Deer. Rabbit. Trout and salmon too, if you smoke them. Mushrooms. You know.

Ren nodded. One week.

All right.

They stood there, each waiting to see if the other had anything else to say. When Ren stayed silent Barlow opened his mouth, ready to speak about something—probably the soldiers again, almost definitely the soldiers—but as Ren saw his lips part she turned and walked away. She left him by the rock and pushed into the trees, treading a trail marked only in her head: stones, moss, logs and cones, connected by the carpet of needles and her memory and nothing more. A trail that couldn't be followed. Behind her, Barlow hefted the skins and turned to the lower slope.

She raced the dropping sun through the trees, walking slow, firm. Up the slope she climbed, on dark grass, over scree fields, through lit clearings and across cold creeks, surrounded always by the towering pines as their needles slid and crunched beneath her fresh boots. Other trees jostled upwards in places— craggy spruces, spreading beeches and the patchwork trunks of skinny, twiggy birches. She'd learned to recognise them all, even the slender silver firs that at first had seemed almost indistinguishable from the mountain pines until she saw how, at greater heights, they stood tall and lonely and noble. But it was the pines that dominated the slopes, in groves and clusters that to Ren were endless and ever welcome.

After an hour she began following the course of a steep stream, at times using her hands to pull herself over the rocks and roots that bordered the water. For another hour she climbed like this: careful, tiring work, avoiding the icy stream, scraping palm skin, birthing blisters against the leather of her boots. The sun fell further and the trees dropped in height. Finally she tacked away from the water. At a sharp angle she picked her way through the forest, and from there it was only a few minutes before she stopped at a clearing beside a high, sheer cliff.

This clearing wasn't like the others lower on the mountain. Where they featured long grass, flat mushrooms and scattered stones, this one was neat and free of wildness. Logs sat at its extremities, and in one corner a patch of ploughed soil shot rows of foreign vegetation upwards. It ended beside the cliff, where a black cave was gouged into the rock face. Inside the cave's mouth, where the diameter narrowed, an uneven wall of logs and sticks, caked with mud and clay, was wedged against the rock. An opening in this wall revealed nothing of the dark interior.

Ren stopped. She drew in the cold high air, its clearing resin scent, and began mentally preparing herself for the night ahead. She needed to drink water, to store the seeds on a dry ledge in her cave, to build a fire by twisting firesticks over cottony tinder. She needed to take her boots off and let her fresh blisters breathe. She needed to eat yams and dried deer meat, and she needed to rest, to lie down, to pull the warm itch of the new blanket up to her chin and sleep.

But she couldn't focus. Her mind wouldn't settle on any one task; her thoughts kept dancing back to the same thing: soldiers. Gun-gripping, fast-marching, unsmiling soldiers, and everything she knew soldiers did and meant. Food, she told herself. Water. Rest. Sleep.

The sun fell behind the mountain. Stars winked bright above her. She felt her pulse trip, her lungs pump. Black boots kicked at the backs of her eyes.

IN THE FIVE years since she'd come to the mountain, Ren had almost died on many occasions. Early on, starvation nearly killed her. Then she nearly died of malnutrition, and the fevers and sickness that came with it. She nearly froze. In a cool, happy stream she nearly drowned. She was nearly gored by a boar, nearly kicked to death by a cornered buck. She nearly poisoned herself with hemlock tea. She nearly fell from a cliff three times, and narrowly missed being crushed by tumbling rocks on many others. All her preparations, her research, all the books she'd read: none of it prepared her for the sheer rush of death that comes with being in the wilderness.

But she did not die, thanks to the shelter she found in the cave, to the foraging and survival skills she cobbled together, to her thick vein of stubbornness. And mostly she didn't die because of Barlow.

She had met him a few weeks after she arrived. She had not yet discovered the cave, and was wandering between shelters, eating her supplies, coming to the realisation that the mountain was going to kill her. On a low slope she saw him with his son foraging for mushrooms, maybe nuts. She saw that he moved slowly, calmly, that he was careful with his footsteps and voice, that he was patient and kind towards the boy, a loud spinning top of a child. Soon they stopped foraging and went back to the village, and Ren felt something hook in her chest as she watched them leave.

Days later she saw him again in the meadow, again with his son. She watched and waited, wondering if they would climb higher. The third time she saw him he was alone, angling for trout with a bamboo pole. He caught a single fish in an hour of casting, and as he packed his bag and turned to leave Ren stepped out from behind a tree, revealing herself without planning to, without thinking about it. He turned; he was coming towards her; she could have stayed hidden but something flicked in her head, a snap of loneliness or need, a snap that travelled all the way to her hip, her knees, and she stepped out before him.

If he was surprised—and he must have been surprised—he didn't show it. He greeted her and asked no personal questions. They spoke about nothing in particular for a while before Ren, conscious of his meagre haul, offered him a handful of the milk-cap mushrooms she'd been collecting. He put them in a side pocket of his backpack, then opened another section and pulled something out, which he offered to Ren. It looked like a piece of wool. After a pause she took it, feeling beneath her fingers the fibre, warm and soft. She stretched it out and saw that it was a woollen hat.

For the mushrooms, Barlow said. And for winter.

It set a simple precedent. They would meet at a large rock in the pines and trade in ways that kept Ren alive, although Barlow never admitted that these trades were weighted in her favour. For mushrooms and berries he traded a rod of steel to sharpen her knife. For a crown of antlers she found on a buck skeleton he gave her a head torch and a pack of batteries. Once she began catching deer in her traps she began asking for things in advance—boots, vitamins and vegetable seeds.

Ren knew that most of these trades were more beneficial to her—a basket of nuts was never a fair swap for a pair of fleece gloves—but she chose not to let her pride get in the way of these meetings, their connection. And sometimes the trades did go

22

in Barlow's favour: once she found a large angular rock that gave off a strange glow, with multiple points of light, varying in colour from white to pink to yellow, glittering out of its pocked surface. She gave it to Barlow in exchange for a tube of disinfectant cream. As his hand closed around the rock she saw his eyes, usually calm and guarded, gleam with wild knowledge. He stammered a thanks, asked if she knew what it was, offered to give her more for it, much more, but she refused. She did not mind, and she did not need more.

He never asked why she was living on the mountain, where she had come from. And Ren never asked him anything about what he did, how he lived, if he had a wife and if that wife was the mother of his son, even though she found herself wondering about this, late at night and in the glow of morning.

They didn't talk about his son, either; she had asked Barlow not to bring him to their meetings. Of all the people she did not want to be around, children were at the top of the list: children and young men, even one that seemed as harmless and light-hearted as the boy she'd seen zooming about on the slopes. She knew what young men could do, no matter how inane they appeared, how joyful and innocent. She knew how they could change and be changed. She knew in her head and blood and hands, and she wanted none of it—none at all, never again.

REN WOKE UP hot. Sweat was sliding down the grooves of her ribs. She wasn't used to the new blanket's thickness, the density of its warmth. In the darkness she threw it off, stretched her legs and arms before standing up, wandering to her door of branches and out into the clearing.

The sun was up, the morning warm. At the stream she drank straight from the water, lying flat, dipping her chin in the current. The water sloshed in her stomach, shaking up her hunger, so she went back and grabbed some dried deer meat from one of the ledges at the back of the cave. Later on she would prepare a meal: usually yams and whatever other vegetables she'd grown, a handful of native thyme and more strips of tough meat, boiled in a metal pot she'd received from Barlow. During the day she might snack on nuts or berries, but this was usually enough: scraps of meat in the morning, and a pot of watery stew later on.

She returned to the stream to fill a dented metal bottle with water. A weak breeze touched her cheeks. The stream gurgled. A steadiness came over her. It wasn't until she began thinking about the rest of the day, about what she needed to do, that she remembered the soldiers.

There was nothing she could do. They might leave; they might already have gone; but once she remembered them she couldn't chase them from her thoughts.

She decided to spend the day being as active as possible, using tasks and work to keep her mind occupied. Her blisters throbbed, so she pulled on two pairs of socks before sliding on her new boots and setting off to the east. She walked through the forest, sticking to patches of shade and wherever possible stepping on stones—a habit that reduced signs of her passing.

Soon she reached a creek that was wider than the stream by her cave. She wandered down its length, stopping at various points near small gullies she'd dug into the dirt beside the course of the water. She'd placed logs and rocks at critical points in the stream that channelled water into these gullies—water that was occasionally followed by unknowing trout. The gullies curved back into lower parts of the stream, where they were fenced off by sticks Ren had jammed into the riverbed, allowing water to pass through, but not fish.

This time there were no trout in her traps. She reset her waterways, using larger logs, and walked on. As she passed through the forest she stopped to pick up mushrooms, nuts and handfuls of the freshest, most fragrant pine needles, but mostly her stride was straight and fast. At the base of a rocky field she tacked south, coming eventually to a faint path in the trees. It was a deer trail. She stopped at a low bend, where the path wound past the thick trunk of an old pine. Here was another of her traps: a device of strained saplings, string and sharpened sticks. A spring-spear trap, or something like it; she'd memorised the design from a survival book she'd read before she came to the mountain.

It had been triggered. Leaves and dirt had been kicked over the trail, a tuft of fur stuck to one of the spikes, and a smear of rust-red blood ran down the wooden barb. She knelt down to reset it, taking care to position her body behind the spikes. The sapling bent under her grip. She reached for the string, straining the wood, tensing her arms, holding her breath with effort, when she heard rustling foliage. Footsteps. Voices.

The sounds were coming from a gully below her. She released the sapling slowly, leaving the trap unset, and lay flat on the ground, her body obscured by the tree but with a clear view of the gully. A minute passed. The noises grew louder, more frequent, and then their source was revealed: one, two, then five soldiers pushed through the trees about thirty metres away.

They were wearing standard camouflage clothing and rifles slung low on their shoulders. They were young men with fresh faces, red cheeks, bored eyes, moving easily and loudly in a loose column—all but for the soldier at the rear, who was a woman. Unlike the men she was treading softly, roving her eyes over the trees and not speaking. Her careful, elegant movements reminded Ren of dancers she'd seen, professional ones. Where the young men crashed, she flowed like water. The men were wearing army caps, but her head was uncovered, revealing a high auburn ponytail. Her lightly tanned face was unlined and expressionless, as if the world held no interest to her—as if the high trees, the rich scent, the clear streams and the looming dark cliffs were all unremarkable, not worth remembering.

The way she moved, the way she took it all in: Ren couldn't stop looking at her. The others were simply soldiers, like the ones she'd known before she left the city. Dangerous, even terrifying at times, but just soldiers: not unique or noticeable beyond the things they did, the things they were allowed and ordered to do. But this blank-faced woman, looking at so much and being affected by none of it: Ren had never seen a soldier like her. And then, still staring at her, at her high, smooth cheekbones and the sheen of sweat on her forehead, Ren had another thought, one that came unbidden and unwelcome: this woman was young enough to be her daughter.

The soldiers stopped. Ren dropped her head. When she looked back up they had turned to face the young woman, who was speaking to them—words that Ren couldn't hear. When she finished they spread into a circle, put down their packs, and began slugging water from bottles and eating bars fished from their pockets.

So she was in charge, Ren thought. Some kind of officer. It made sense—she wasn't sure why, but it did. The intrigue that had been bubbling at the back of her neck fizzed higher, brighter, matched only by the fear that had been brewing beside it: fear that grew larger the longer she lay there, watching the young woman take small sips from a shining steel bottle.

REN THOUGHT THESE soldiers would keep searching, that they'd find her, but over the next week she didn't see them again, and her life followed its usual routine. Seven trout swam into her rejigged fish traps; she whacked them dead on river rocks and took them back to the cave to clean and smoke. She planted a new crop of wild yams, fertilising the soil with trout guts, ash and armfuls of dry leaves, before drenching the soil with water. One hot morning she carried all of her clothes to a stream at the base of a small waterfall. There she scrubbed away the sweat and dirt that she was always collecting, using a flat stone and the palms of her hard hands. After she'd washed these clothes she took off the set she was wearing and scrubbed them as well, before standing under the torrent, numbing herself clean.

Under the cold fall of the water, she felt pangs of age. She pulled a handful of hair in front of her face, and studied its lack of colour. It was closer to white than grey—a change she hadn't noticed. Her hands ached. Her knees throbbed. She ran a hand over her neck, her waist, her thighs, feeling her lack of fat and the firmness of her muscles. She was still strong, she told herself, as strong as she needed to be. She stared at a distant tree and counted its pine cones, confirming that her eyes still worked. It occurred to her that she might be feeling her years because of the young soldier she'd seen, so swift and sure in her movements. The water slapped at her back. She stepped out, got dressed, and took off to her cave in a fast march.

Every day she checked the deer trap where she'd seen the soldiers. It was still set, taut, empty. On the sixth day she leaned down behind it to inspect the tripwire, making sure it was at the right height. Her hand reached over the trap, brushing the wire, the lightest graze of skin on twine, but that was all it took: the arm of the trap exploded outwards, whipping into her upper arm. A wooden spike stabbed into her bicep, a quick, clean puncture, before jagging down the muscle as she reflexively pulled her arm back. Pain burned through her. Ren swore. She grabbed her arm and blew huge breaths through her nostrils. She crouched down and groaned through her teeth as blood streamed over her forearm, her wrist, through the webbing of her fingers to pour into the soil beneath her.

There was no sound, at least none that she could hear. Not even the ravens, usually ever-present, cawed above. After a minute passed she grasped the spike with her free hand, felt for a straight angle and, with a sharp inhalation of breath, pulled it loose from her flesh. A feeling of release washed through her, then of shock, and all the while pain still bounced in her nerves. Sudden dizziness pushed her to the ground. She looked at the wound. Blood was flowing freely from it—not in time with her pulse, but steadily, and too much, far too much. She grabbed a handful of leaves, jammed them against the jagged hole and began staggering back to the cave.

By the time she made it there she was woozy and sick, and blood had soaked through the leaves. She leaned into the stream near the cave and washed away the drying blood and soggy nature. Cold water flushed through the wound, and she gasped. She clambered back to her feet, into the cave, found her first-aid kit. She pulled the cap off a tube of disinfectant cream and smeared it around the mouth of the wound, then rolled a thick white bandage around her arm, even as blood continued to ooze out of it. She fastened the bandage with a tight knot.

She counted to ten. Her wound felt hot; her whole arm did. Everywhere else, she was cold.

Ren knew she needed to eat, so she tore into a handful of nuts and dried trout, as much as she could stomach. Then she knew she should rest, stop moving, let her blood clot, her flesh relax. But as soon as she sat down, sinking into her needle-bed, she remembered that tonight was her scheduled meeting with Barlow. She stood back up, gasping and grunting. Outside, the light was fading. She grabbed four smoked trout, threw them in her backpack and lurched off down the mountain, trying to hold her arm still and straight, but failing; the bandage slipped. Fresh blood ran down her skin.

Barlow was waiting for her by the rock. He looked even thinner than usual, his wiry body stooped and tired. But when he saw her, his beard was broken open by his usual wide smile, and his gentle friendliness showed itself in the crease of his eyes. She stopped a few metres away from him, out of breath, sweat smearing her face, injured arm behind her back. He looked harder at her, and the happiness on his face disappeared.

Is everything okay?

I'm fine.

He peered around her back, seeing the arm, the poorly wrapped wound, the bandage splotched and crusted with blood.

You don't look fine.

Ren straightened up, slowed her breathing. The trees had taken on a glossy shimmer.

It's just a scratch. We don't need to talk about it.

Barlow frowned.

Okay.

He turned back to look at the path he'd walked up.

You remember those soldiers I told you about?

Yes.

They're still here. Every day they head up the mountain. Have you seen them?

Ren nodded. Her throat was dry, her skin tight.

They keep asking questions. Strange ones, about old stories from the region. Myths. Nonsense. Things nobody believes any more.

Ren shrugged.

Frustration contorted Barlow's face.

Well. I thought I'd let you know. And another thing— they're following anyone who leaves the village. Two of them tried to follow me tonight. I lost them fairly easily, but still. It's not safe. I don't think we should meet again until they've gone.

Ren didn't move.

Fine.

Will you be okay?

He tried to look again at her arm.

I have nothing on me, but I'll try to get some more bandages to you. Antibiotics, if I can find some.

Ren was going to ask him how he'd deliver these things, how he'd find her, but her bones and joints were aching, and her wound had taken on a fierce throb, so she just said: I'll be fine. See you when they're gone.

Then she turned and walked away, ignoring the words Barlow shout-whispered at her back, words she couldn't make out.

It wasn't until she was halfway back to the cave that she

realised she was being followed. On a better day, with sharper wits and more energy, she would have picked up on it straight away. As it was, it took the sound of a rock slipping into a stream to alert her. The splash was followed by a rustle: someone hiding behind a bush or tree. Ren didn't turn around. She stretched her back, as if she was tired—and she was, she was exhausted, but not in the way she was feigning—and began moving in a zigzag pattern, tacking north here, east there, creating an unpredictable pattern through the trees. She picked up her pace until she reached a boulder field, which she hobble-sprinted into, throwing herself behind the largest stone in sight.

She waited. Her arm was approaching agony, and she was sure that at any moment she would vomit. But she didn't, not even when she heard the sound of boots walking towards her. They stopped on the other side of the boulder. Two voices spoke in hushed sentences she couldn't make out before the boots crunched and turned. The sound of receding footsteps was all Ren could hear; still there were no birds, no ravens, no whoosh of wind on branch. She waited half an hour before inching out from behind the rock and slinking back into the trees.

The mountain was vast and the forests were thick, but now they knew she was there, they would eventually find her. This should have terrified her, but all she could think of was that she'd forgotten to show Barlow the trout; that she'd hauled four fish up and down the mountain for nothing; that it was the first time they'd arranged to meet, and not traded a thing.

WHENEVER SHE MOVED the wound spat pain through her: bright, harsh jolts that emptied her lungs and jellied her knees. She could no longer travel far. Hunting, foraging, cleaning, gathering—all were now vastly more difficult, if she could do them at all. Creating fire was impossible.

If the soldiers were looking for her, she didn't notice. For four days she couldn't venture past her clearing. Unable to cook, she grazed through her stores of dried meat and nuts. She slept a lot, or tried to. She unwound the bandage daily and washed it in the stream, before dabbing more disinfectant around the wound. She couldn't tell if it was getting better. Blood still oozed from the gape in her flesh, and the muscle didn't seem to be knitting itself back together. At least it wasn't infected, she told herself. At least she wouldn't have to cut the whole thing off.

Most of her time was spent sitting outside the cave, watching the wind play with the tops of the pines, waiting for cones to fall to the ground. Counting the crashing cones, watching for changes in the wind, listening for intrusions in the soundscape: these were the only things she had to occupy her. Locked in this quiet, almost meditative state, she succumbed to memory.

First came images: a long beach, a fraying palm, a tide frothed with foam, slow-changing traffic lights beside a string of faded shopfronts. Suddenly she could feel the coastal city she was from: the salt twisting through her hair, the granular itch of sand on her skin, the lancing heat of asphalt under a bare foot, the squint of sunlight on salt water, the tight sting of burnt skin.

And there was more, more than mere glimpses and physical sensations; scenes played through her mind, fast and loud. Shoving a lawnmower over a tussock of high blond grass, feeling the whirring blade catch on a rock, hearing its roar peal out into the suburb. Ordering a second bottle of wine—or was it a third?—in a restaurant while familiar faces and voices swam around the table, laughter bouncing as duck fat slicked the inside of her cheek. Sleeping on a thick bed, not alone, waking up with heat and flesh and hair pressed against her back. Sitting in her car outside a school, the radio shouting ads and music as she waited, watching the children swirl through the low iron gates towards her.

And these were just the start, just the surface, the smallest slivers of her old life reaching up to scratch at her while she sat, her back resting against a hard cliff, her arm throbbing hot as the wind rushed through the pines and her breath grew shorter, sharper, faster.

SOMEONE FOUND HER on the afternoon of the third day after the accident. She was sitting in her usual spot beside the cave when she heard them approaching. Their footsteps were soft, not cracking any sticks, not disturbing any undergrowth. She looked in the direction of the sound and saw only trees. The footsteps stopped. She lurched up, ran inside the cave and came back out clutching her knife. Her tracker was waiting for her, standing in the centre of the clearing.

It was Barlow's son. A slender boy of ten or so, with brown hair and bony extremities. She had never been this close to him, had never realised how much he looked like Barlow. The knobbly joints, the narrowness in the cheeks, the chin. A wary kindness leaking out of him, a tinge of innocence or good intentions. She felt a sudden and powerful desire to be near his father. She lowered the knife.

She couldn't remember his name, if Barlow had ever told her what it was.

He was holding a palm out towards her. In his other hand he held a small calico bag. His eyes were wide but his face was still, his posture hunched, as if she were a spooked deer he was trying to placate.

She spoke first.

Who followed you?

Nobody.

How do you know?

He motioned at the mountain, at the trees.

I grew up here. I can tell. They didn't even see me leave the village.

How did you find me?

Dad said you'd be up here somewhere.

Why didn't he come? Why did he send you?

The boy shrugged.

I'm smaller. There was more chance I wouldn't be noticed.

And you're sure you weren't?

He nodded. He looked around the clearing, at the cave, at her garden.

I've been looking for two days. I followed the streams until I found a trail.

There is no trail.

He looked at the ground.

Sorry. It just seemed like a path.

A moment passed until Ren spoke again.

You should leave.

I will. I'm sorry. Dad just wanted me to bring you this.

He took a few steps towards her and dipped his free hand into the calico bag, fishing something out. It was a wad of white gauzy material.

Dad said you'd need these.

Then he pulled a small glass bottle from the bag.

I'm not sure what these are, but he said they'd help.

Ren held out her hand, and the boy placed the bottle into her palm. She held it up to her eye to read the label. She didn't recognise the brand, or most of the words, but she could tell that they were antibiotics. She held the bandages and the pills back out to the boy.

I don't have anything to trade.

The boy backed away, the bag in front of him like a shield.

You don't need to give me anything. Dad said you'd make

up for it. A few deerskins, he told me to tell you. When you get them.

Ren looked at the things in her hand. At the boy. Back at the bandages and pills.

Thank you. Thank your father for me.

You're welcome. I'll tell him.

He glanced again around the clearing.

I better be going. I'm only supposed to have been gone for a day.

Yes.

She thought she should thank him again, but she'd already done it once. She'd forgotten how to reiterate things, how to press with emotion.

The boy nodded before turning and setting off on the path Ren always took when she left the clearing, the path she had been sure didn't exist.

She went to the stream, where she unwound her current bandage, washed her wound, applied disinfectant cream and tied on one of the new ones. The fabric was tight and fresh against her arm, and smelt of something old and familiar to her: clean, starchy sheets. She shook the memory away. The pain was still there, still throbbing hot, so after hesitating she opened the bottle of antibiotics and pushed two of them into her mouth, along with a handful of stream water. The pills felt huge and unwieldy in her throat, but she got them down.

This swallowing suddenly and unexpectedly filled her with a sense of success. She thought: I can swallow pills; I'm not so weak; what else can I do? She walked to her fire pit and grabbed a thin stick before sitting down next to a branch riddled with blackened holes. She positioned the stick so its point was poking into the flattest part of the branch and began twisting it between her palms. Pain lanced out from her wound, but she felt strong, angry. She twisted harder, running her hands down the stick and bringing them back to the top, grimacing with effort and agony as her wound screamed and her arms ached and the stick swivelled. She thought she would run out of energy, or that she'd pass out, but then a thin curl of smoke plumed out of the branch. She increased her speed, a final furious effort, before twists of smoking wood shavings began screwing up beside the point of the stick. She threw it aside and scraped these smoking twists into a clump of dried leaves and bark fibre, which she cupped in her hands and began blowing at with long, slow breaths. The smoke increased, billowing up into her face, stinging her eyes and dragging coughs from her throat before orange flames leapt out of the tinder, nearly burning her hands.

She tipped the flames into the pit and added more leaves, then twigs; then, as the fire danced higher, thicker sticks. When it was crackling evenly she filled her cooking pot at the stream and set it on the coals to boil, adding dried mountain herbs, some stunted yams and two potatoes she pulled from her garden.

An hour later she was eating hot food and drinking thin, warm broth for the first time in days. The starchy food and sloshing water churned with the antibiotics in her stomach, making her dizzy. Above her the sky was dark and clear, a navy sheet shot through with stars, and with fuzzy clarity she remembered that she loved the mountain. The scrubbed, endless sky; the sweet-clearing scent; the tossing wind and the bending trees and the high peaks and the running, freezing glassiness of the streams. The world felt new to her again, fresh and wild and kind, and she was filled with gladness that she'd come here, that she was living like this and that she would die like this, surrounded by nothing but trees and moss, with fresh air blowing across her skin.

It would be so nice to sleep out here beneath the stars, she thought, so quiet and easy. But eventually she hauled herself back into the cave, as the coals were glowing low, winking orange into the trees.

THE NEXT MORNING she woke up feeling better than she had in days. Her arm still hurt if she moved it, but the throbbing had stopped. Her lungs felt strong; her body was rested; even her mind was clear. She felt a renewed sense of purpose, of capability. Then she smelled smoke.

She rushed to the front of the cave, filled with flashing thoughts of fire, of coals, of the stream and how much water she could carry. But when she burst into the clearing she saw that she wouldn't need to dash about, that there was no emergency. There was a fire, but someone was tending it. Someone in front of the pit, blowing on the embers, adding twigs and tinder. Someone with a small frame, wearing a uniform of brown and green, an auburn ponytail held high above her skull.

The soldier was crouching low, with her back to the cave. Ren hesitated; she didn't know if she should run to grab her knife or just run, as far and fast as she could. As these thoughts cycled through her, the soldier called out.

Good morning.

Her voice was soft, deep, deeper than Ren had expected. She stood up—slow, elegant, as if standing was part of her morning stretching routine—and turned. Ren saw the same smooth face she'd noticed when she first saw the soldiers: the calm expression, the lineless skin. Again the thought came, unbidden: she's young enough to be my daughter.

Sorry for startling you.

Ren stood still, wary. The soldier waited. Eventually Ren found her voice.

What do you want?

A pistol was hanging at the soldier's hip. The sight of it—the snug holster, the jet-black metal—made her conscious of the veins in her neck, the blood pulsing at her temple.

The soldier smiled.

Some help.

I can't help you.

Why don't you come over here?

She motioned at the logs by the fire.

I won't hurt you.

I'm fine here.

The soldier turned back to the fire and sat down on a log beside it. She grabbed a stick and began poking at the coals. Ren was going to say something else, to tell her to leave, to shout it, but the soldier was clearly not planning on leaving. Ren went back into the cave and picked up her knife. For a moment she stood there, clutching the rubber grip, breathing heavily, trying to slow her pulse. Then she walked back out into the clearing, making sure her spine was straight and her strides were sure, and sat on a log opposite the soldier.

She glanced up as Ren sat down, noticing the knife without reacting. A moment passed before she spoke.

Five years? Six?

What?

How long you've been up here, said the soldier.

She gestured at the clearing, at Ren's garden.

I'd say you've been here half a decade. I suppose it makes sense. The coup happened about five years ago. You aren't the only one who fled it.

Ren didn't answer.

The soldier gazed up at the trees, at the rich blue field

above them, and drew a long, deep breath through her nostrils.

I can see why you came here. Why wouldn't you run some-where this beautiful?

I'm not running.

No, I guess not.

She exhaled, turned her face away from the canopy. Her mouth shifted slightly, as she looked at Ren, refocusing.

Boys, she said. Always so confident.

Ren didn't respond.

So noisy, continued the soldier. Even when they think they're being quiet.

Something was thrashing inside Ren's throat. She saw Barlow's son's face in her clearing, the wary kindness, and she saw Barlow's face, warm and thin and bright.

Don't hurt him.

The soldier frowned.

Why would we hurt him? He's a child.

She kept poking the fire, needling her stick into a coal until sparks spat out.

Ren waited, watching the fire grow, until she felt calm enough to speak again.

Who are you?

The soldier placed the stick on the ground. She ran a hand over her hair, up into the ponytail.

My name is Lieutenant Harker. And as I said, I'm here to ask for your help.

I live here alone. I don't bother anyone; I don't go anywhere. There's nothing I can help you with.

Harker leaned back onto her hands, another movement

that seemed more like a practised stretch, a ritualistic movement.

You're wrong. You're probably the only person who can.

Ren tried to keep her face as placid as Harker's, but she couldn't. Her eyes narrowed, her shoulders bunched.

Harker kept talking.

We're after something that lives here. And seeing as you're up here alone, and you don't go anywhere, you're the perfect person to help us find it.

What are you talking about?

Harker stood up and leaned down to touch her boots, showing the back of her head to Ren, her hair dropping low.

We know. We know it's up here.

Nothing's up here.

Harker straightened up. She stared hard and straight at Ren.

The bird. The one that comes from the clouds. The rain heron.

A long pause followed. Ren wanted to laugh, but nothing came out. Finally, she said: That's just a story.

I know.

A fairy tale, Ren continued, willing her voice to take on an edge of incredulity, of sarcasm, thinking she could gain power by doing this, by showing humour at this absurd idea. I didn't think soldiers believed in fairy tales.

What we believe is irrelevant. It's not our job to believe. It's our job to follow orders.

Harker pulled an arm across her chest.

And our orders are to come to this mountain, to capture the bird, and to return it to our superiors.

43

Flames were jumping to the height of Harker's knees. The clearing fell silent, save for the crack and spit of the fire.

I can't help crazy people.

Are you sure?

Ren wanted to call her crazy again, to say that nobody had seen a rain heron in centuries, if they'd ever seen one at all, that it was just a story told in schools. But she stayed quiet.

Harker kept looking at her, as if expecting Ren to continue. After a few moments she blew out a long sound of frustration, or maybe sadness. A tiny fold appeared in her forehead.

A shame.

She reached into a pocket of her trousers and retrieved a small bottle. Ren blinked. It was her antibiotic pills, the ones Barlow's son had given her.

A shame, Harker repeated. She opened the bottle and poured the antibiotics into the fire, then turned and walked out of the clearing, merging into the green.

Ren rushed forward. Flames danced around the little oblong pills, cocooning them in heat and harsh light before swooping over their smooth bodies, turning them ashen. She reached into the pit but instantly jerked her hand back, blisters already forming on a burn, as the chemicals inside the pills began to fizz and bubble up and out of each pale shape—black-rimmed bubbles that swelled and burst and reformed until all that was left of the medicine was a small acrid plume of sooty smoke, rising to mingle with the air of the forest.

THE THROBBING RETURNED, at first in pumps, then in waves. Ren kept applying the antiseptic cream, but the tube soon ran out, and the torn lips of her wound turned scarlet, swollen, hot to touch. Yellow-white pus began oozing from the depths of her muscle, carrying an oily, sick scent.

Three days after she ran out of cream Ren tried to unwrap her bandage, only to find that the drying pus had fused to the wound. She lay by the creek, submerging her arm in the water until the gauzy fabric unglued itself from her flesh. Thick threads of pus swam away down the stream. Her wound rang out with pain and rot.

She could have gone to the village to beg for more antibiotics, but she knew the soldiers would be patrolling the lower slopes. She had no way of contacting Barlow, and even if she could, she didn't want to. They knew his son had come to see her; any further connection would only bring him harm. Without medicine, she should at least have rested, but her stores of food had dwindled dangerously—all she had left were a few half-grown, unharvested vegetables and a handful of stale nuts. So, despite the infection, despite the mind-blanking stabs that now shot through her left side whenever she made even a slightly rough movement, she got up each day and went foraging.

Every movement was awkward, every chore a fresh agony; every choice was a compromise between what she could manage and what would keep her alive. Gathering nuts, mushrooms, herbs and fresh pine needles was okay, but she'd never relied on these things for more than a third of her diet. Now she grabbed as much as she could, and while it was enough to feed her for a few days, she soon went through all the easily collectable food in the area. Checking traps was possible, but resetting them wasn't; her arm couldn't take the intricacy and strain her snares required. From her existing set-ups she managed to snag a few rabbits and a single fish, with no hope of catching any more.

Worse, her endeavours on the mountain were being sabotaged. At first she wasn't sure of it—she thought her snapped snares and displaced fish gullies were caused by weather or animal interference. Then she returned from a brief outing to find her vegetable patch churned and smashed. Her zucchinis, potatoes, pumpkins and yams had been yanked out and stomped into the rocky soil beside the dark loam. She knelt, trying to reclaim as much edible material as she could from the boot prints, and saw tiny white granules littered through the remnants of the patch. A smell rose to her nostrils—a smell that carried scenes of her old life, of the beach, of a rusting breeze and crusting residue. They had salted her garden.

Wet rage welled up inside her, big, overwhelming, but not as big as the hunger aching in her gut—a hunger that drove her back into the forest.

After a half-hour of maddened searching, her movements not even hinting at quietness or stealth, she came across a patch of blackberries, the vines weighed down by dark fruit. She fell upon the bush, ignoring the thorns that pricked her fingers, her wrists, as she ripped the berries free and shoved them into her mouth. The rich flavour lanced her tongue. Blood raced through her veins, juice smeared at the corners of her mouth, and still she kept eating. For ten minutes she gorged, stopping only to burp and breathe, until finally she leaned back, dizzy and sick and full, to see that Lieutenant Harker was watching her.

She was propped against a tree, arms crossed. A thoughtful expression hung on her face—a sucking of the cheeks, a pinching of the brow.

I thought you would've found this bush days ago. We've known about it for a week.

Ren didn't respond. Harker pointed at her wound.

That doesn't look like fun.

Again Ren didn't speak. The fruit was bubbling in her stomach. She had eaten too much, too fast. It had brought on a wooziness, which, coupled with the ever-present throb of her arm, made her want to close her eyes and lie down. Only Harker's presence kept her upright.

Now she came closer. Ren could see a spray of freckles across her nose and cheeks: the work of the mountain sun, she thought, and then she was thinking of girls at the beach, of children, of sharp shells and rip currents and bird calls.

Let me help you.

Harker's voice had lowered but her tone was the same, flat and neutral.

I don't like doing this. We'll fix your arm. We'll leave.

She crouched down before Ren.

Just help us find the bird.

Ren pulled herself into a straighter sitting position.

I bet they think you're too young.

Harker's face remained still, touched only by the freckles.

They say it, don't they? That you're too young. And here you are. Up a mountain, chasing a fairy tale.

Harker stood up. If she was affected by Ren's words, if anger or shame had crept across her face, Ren didn't see it.

Harker just smoothed her ponytail and stretched her arms high above her head, arching her back.

This ends when you let it.

Then she was gone, twisting back into the trees with that poise and deftness that somehow bordered on violence.

Five minutes later, Ren heaved herself to her feet, swaying and grunting, and began making her way home. It took much longer than usual, and though she was filled with the energy of the berries she was also battling the sickness they had awoken in her. She went slowly, pausing, sucking in deep breaths whenever she felt like vomiting, not wanting to lose her meal. As she reached her clearing another wave of nausea washed through her, and she steadied herself against a tree. Fresh, pine-thick air filled her lungs, and the bile backed down her throat.

As she leaned, Ren realised that she could feel something foreign beneath her fingers. Where there should have been rough bark, she felt smooth wood and viscous stickiness. She turned to face the tree and saw a wide, neat wound in the trunk, spreading out from beneath her hand. Sap was leaking in glossy rivulets down the naked timber. She circled the tree to see the full extent of the damage. A full ring of bark had been cut off, completely separating one section of the trunk from the other. Ren backed away and turned to study the tree behind her. It, too, had been relieved of a ring of bark, as had the one beside it, and the next one, and the next. She staggered onwards, seeing rings of raw wood on the trunks, matching strips of bark on the ground, on every tree within sight of her home.

It was only then, faced with not just her own starvation and death but with the destruction of the forest around her, with the killing of the trees and the loss of their shade and scent and swamping greenness, that she began to consider telling Harker the truth: that the rumours were true. That a bird made of rain did live on the mountain. That she had seen it.

IT HAPPENED WHEN she was a child, the first time she'd come to the mountain. She'd been camping with her grandmother. They had spent the time rambling through the trees, building campfires, cooking flatbread damper, hunting for waterfalls and staring at the stars, and Ren had assumed they'd continue doing this until the end of the trip. But on the evening before they were to leave, as Ren was collecting firewood, her grandmother interrupted her.

Let's do something special.

They put water bottles, trail snacks and warm outer clothes into a daypack and headed further up the mountain. First they went through the forest, along broad trails that were easy to follow. When the sun began falling, sending the hazy light of dusk slanting through the trees, Ren asked when they'd be arriving at the special place, when they'd do or see the special thing, but her grandmother marched on, her pack swaying with each step.

They climbed higher, steeper, and eventually the trees shrunk in size and thinned out, dwarfing into tiny pines that may as well have been bushes. Ren was tired. She had already spent the day running, hunting, fishing. Now she began losing track of time. She dragged her eyes up from her feet to see that they were on a rocky slope, not following any trail she could make out, and with barely any light left to guide their way. She asked if they could turn around, but again her grandmother did not answer.

The night deepened. They trudged on, ever upwards. Ren's thighs and heels ached. The wind picked up, bringing a biting chill to their climb. Her grandmother passed her a jacket, but still they did not stop. Just as Ren thought that the air had become too thin to breathe, that the wind would cut the skin from her cheeks, that she could go no further, her grandmother reached back to take her hand while pointing forward with another, and she saw it: a great wall of smooth rock, jutting up from the slope, rising high into the clouds above them.

This is it, Ren thought. Some kind of rock formation. We have climbed all the way up here to look at a geological oddity we could have seen in daylight. But her grandmother pulled her forward, and Ren saw that the wall of rock was not whole: there was an opening in its face, a dark crevice roughly the shape and size of a crouching human.

She knew instantly that they were going in there, and that she wasn't going to object. The maw of the opening was pitch dark, but when her grandmother ducked her head and pushed inside Ren didn't hesitate to follow. After a few minutes of scrabbling through the darkness, following the sounds of her grandmother's pack scraping against the rock, they emerged in a long, narrow crevasse. Dark cliffs shot high on either side. There was no wind, and the sky above them was clear. Bright stars shone down with fierce light. Ren realised they had gone higher than the clouds. They were walking in a canyon on the roof of the world.

Still her grandmother did not speak. The way was tight. They had to hold themselves sideways, sucking in their lungs, wriggling and squeezing through the gaps in the path. Grazes began accumulating on Ren's knees, elbows, shoulders and shins, and the hard walls of the crevasse began to press in.

The night was receding from above her, speeding away and growing smaller as the rock crowded. Her breaths fell short and shallow, and her mind began swimming, until she felt her grandmother's hand knuckle into the folds of her coat and pull her through the final gap.

Ren bent over, heaving deep breaths. Then she straightened up, looked around, and lost the air she'd taken in. Before them the cliffs had abandoned their canyon shape and bulged out into a natural amphitheatre with a wide gap that opened onto a clean view of sky and stars. The ground around them was covered with a thick, verdant moss. Every stone, every surface shone with its dark-green light, somehow visible in the night. The moss gave way in front of them to a small tarn. Its water was still and clear, reflecting the scene around it: the moon, the cliffs, the moss, the sky, even Ren and her grandmother, standing solemnly before it.

Beyond the tarn, at the edge of the clearing, next to the opening in the amphitheatre and presumably above an enormous cliff, was a tree. It was a small, stunted thing, with ancient knots and whorls twisted into its trunk and limbs, as if it had spent millennia folding in on itself. Small, hardened needles sprang forth from its outermost tips, but it was otherwise bare, with grey-white bark coating its gnarled body.

At its highest point, in a clawing crown of branches, sat a bird. It looked like a heron, although it was too big, too blue, too alien. Huge and silent, it was running its long beak through its pale cerulean plumage. Ren watched it groom itself, transfixed by the sight. Water was dripping from the feathers as the bird preened, shedding in a stream of moisture that fell and collected at the base of the tree. She stared, unmoving, until her grandmother's whisper crept into her ear.

Do you see it?

Yes.

Really?

Of course.

It was right there—of course she could see it; why was her grandmother talking now, the worst time to talk, when she'd spent the whole night saying nothing?

Then her grandmother was lifting an arm.

How about now?

Ren followed the line of her arm, looking closer. As if sensing her gaze, the bird launched itself from the tree, trailing rain from its talons. It twirled in the windless air, shaking ice and dew across the clearing and over Ren and her grandmother, drawing from them shivers and shrieks, before falling in a straight, fast dive into the tarn. It disappeared, but it caused no splash, made no ripples. It was as if the bird had become one with the water, rather than sinking beneath its surface.

Ren wiped at her eyes. Something glowed and fizzed inside her.

Her grandmother whispered again.

I told you.

Yes.

Something special.

Yes.

OLD WOMEN DIE, even midnight-mountain-scaling grand-mothers. Ren's had caught pneumonia in the days after they got home. Ren never had the chance to talk to her about what they'd seen, or how her grandmother had known about it. And maybe she never would have—maybe the trip had been too strange, the sight too unreal for Ren ever to bring it up back in the city.

When she'd returned to the mountain as an adult she was so much older. She was also harder, angrier, brimming with sorrow, and less inclined to trust and talk, and she hadn't gone looking for the bird. She'd had food to find, shelter to build; there was no time to climb to the highest peak, to scarper through the wall of rock, not when she was facing freezing nights and imminent starvation. She hadn't gone to the mountain for the rain heron: she'd gone there to escape.

But she remembered the bird, and she remembered where it lived; and five years later she had known that the soldiers were there to find it, as soon as Barlow had told her they'd come to the mountain. She'd also known she wouldn't help them. Not just because they were soldiers, although that was certainly part of it. It was because of Harker.

Ren had seen the way she stalked around the mountain, unmoved by the trees, the air, the staggering slopes and the cellophane streams, the huge and harsh beauty of it all. For Harker, the mountain was no different to a car park, an office, the bottom of the ocean; she would use it, take what she needed, burn it down, dance gracefully in the ashes and never think of it again. Ren could tell: she had seen it in her smooth face, heard it in her placid voice. She knew the type.

Nobody should touch a rain heron, especially not a person who salted gardens, who ringbarked trees. Ren would make sure of it. She would watch Harker leave empty-handed, regardless of the cost. Whatever they did to her, she had survived worse.

TIME WAVERED, SHIMMERED. She could no longer tell whether days were beginning or ending. Most of the time she lay in her cave, not quite asleep or awake, buffeted not just by hunger, thirst and pain but also by visions, memories, half-dreams. Mostly they were scenes of her past life—the sea and the sand, the dinners and the bedrooms, the children rushing out of the school gates—but soon they were crowded by other, more recent apparitions. Lieutenant Harker stretching and flexing in the trees, smoke from burning pills rising around her calves. Harker again, speaking low, calm words that Ren couldn't make out, while her soldiers chewed on tubers they'd ripped from her garden, hard roots splintering in their mouths, cutting their young gums raw and bloody.

And Barlow. Barlow fishing, Barlow speaking, Barlow walking with his son; Barlow's face, and the way it would relax into a smile when they met at the rock. Then his soft, gentle smile began changing. Her sickness and her malnourishment grabbed hold of it and began melding it with other faces, the faces of men she had known and loved and would never see again. Her father, her brothers, her uncles, old friends, lovers, colleagues, men she had known through shops and swimming clubs and daily routines—all these abandoned faces swam in and out of Barlow's, until she could no longer remember which part was truly his, or recognise which face belonged solely to him. He appeared so much to her, yet in this way he began to slip, muddled and watery, and her despair, even in the depths of her sleep, had never been so wild.

One morning or afternoon or evening—or maybe it was the dead of night, the moon and stars shining down on her instead of the yellow sun—she awoke on the grass beside her cave, gripped by a huge thirst. On scabbed knees she crawled to the creek, thinking only of water, of its coldness, of throat-drenching relief. She reached the stream and threw her hands into the current. Her palms filled. She lifted the liquid to her face, opened her wobbling jaw, tilted her neck, and in the moment before she poured the water onto her swollen tongue, she smelled something terrible.

The water fell from her hands. She sniffed again. At first she thought the smell was her infected wound, so she pushed her nose closer to her arm, but it wasn't the source. Her wound exuded its own distinct brand of pus-heavy nasal horror. This new smell was more coppery, more meaty, of flesh closer to vitality than that of her arm.

She held her face down to the surface, which increased the intensity of the smell, and she could see faint clouds of redness in the usually transparent creek. Looking upstream she could spot nothing unusual, so she crawled along the bank, around a sharp dogleg in the waterway. Here the view was less crowded, and she could see all the way up to where the stream ran down the cliff. She could see the high spruces, towering above her ringbarked pines. She could see mossy boulders, patches of swarthy grass, thick bushes. She could see the steep harshness of the cliff: its grand height, its grey-cragging face. And lower down, closer, where the water ran slower, she could see the source of its fouling.

The rent, ragged corpse of a once-great buck was splayed over the centre of the creek. Its legs were crooked, wrong-angled. Its crown of antlers rose from the water, fuzzed with velvet, proud and serene against the greenness of the trees even as the head it sprouted from lay half-crushed in the slow-flowing stream. Where the buck's brow should have been high and strong it was broken and squashed; skull fragments popped out of the thin fur on its face. A grey tongue had fallen from its open jaw. An eye that should have held an amber iris was clouded and milky; the other was submerged in the current.

These wrong legs and this huge, broken head were perhaps the least ruined parts of the buck's body—its flanks and chest and back were torn apart by what looked to Ren like bullet holes. Blood had run and dried from each individual wound, creating a dense pattern of dark-scarlet snakes. But the worst damage had been done to its belly: slashed into the creamy underfur was a jagged, flapping aperture, revealing a red inner gloom. Organs had spilled or been pulled out of this opening: ropey intestines, a loose bag of stomach, liver, spleen and lungs, all artlessly strewn from the wound to the riverbank, making sure no drop of water could flow downstream without touching a piece of the bloating, floating offal.

The smell was huge—meat, death, half-digested grass and organ rot. Ren's throat burned with bile, even as it rasped with thirst. The buck's milk-clouded eye shone pale and bright.

She turned from the corpse, her knees twisting in the dirt, and began crawling back to her cave. She might have a bottle there, still half-full. Or rainwater could have collected in some of the ledges on the rock face. She tried to remember the last time it had rained. At once she could feel water hitting her skin, droplets landing on her arms and shoulders and scalp. She could see grey clouds; she could smell drenched grass; she could hear the patter of a steady downpour; but she could not remember when it had last happened. She opened her eyes, still crawling, to see sunlight falling on the clearing in front of her. There was bound to be water there, somewhere. She crawled on, around the rock face.

Harker was sitting on the ground by her cave. She was flipping a bottle in tight loops, its handle repeatedly landing in her palm. Water moved inside the metal shell, churning with each toss. She must have seen Ren approaching, but she said nothing. She didn't even look up, not even when Ren collapsed a few metres in front of her. It was only when noises began croaking from Ren's throat that Harker ceased flipping the bottle, stood up and walked over to crouch by her.

Pardon?

She'd lowered her face to be near Ren's, but she wasn't looking at her. She was staring out at the ringbarked trees.

I'll do it.

Do what?

The bird. I'll take you to it.

Harker bent her crouch into a kneel. Ren thought she hadn't heard her, so she sucked in another breath, preparing to repeat herself, when she felt something strange: a hand, running down the back of her head in gentle strokes. Ren recoiled at the touch, but she couldn't move as fast or as far as she wanted to. All she could manage was a stiff roll, onto her side, facing Harker, whose hand came to rest on her shoulder. In this position, propped up on a wobbling elbow, Ren saw something even more surprising than the feeling of Harker's hand on her head: she saw her smile.

A wide grin broke open the lieutenant's face, transforming it completely. A new person was crouching there: not a grim, emotionless soldier but a young woman like any other, one who knew happiness, who felt joy. Two rows of straight, snowy teeth glowed out of her mouth. Small creases appeared beside her eyes. Even her eyebrows had risen, as if this happiness was mixed with surprise or relief.

Thank you.

Pleasure lilted her voice upwards. She shifted, sliding from a crouch into a seated position, and somehow in this movement Ren's head came to rest in her lap. Ren struggled, jerking her neck and shoulders, but Harker's hand kept stroking, forcing her into stillness. She flicked open the cap of her bottle, tilted Ren's head upwards and began pouring a trickle of water into her mouth.

Drink.

Ren stopped struggling. She did as she was told and let the water drain down her throat. It was the purest form of relief she'd ever experienced. Harker's hand stroked on, soft yet firm. Ren couldn't summon the energy to fight back or roll away. Nor could she deny the pleasure of it: not just the physical pleasure of a hand softly patting her neck, but the warm, animalistic pleasure of feeling safe, protected. Flashes of her childhood came to her, of her mother holding her like this as she lay on the couch, watching television.

Water kept flowing into her mouth. She wondered how she looked, a grey-haired woman, ill and delirious, with her head in the lap of someone who could be her daughter, who was touching her in the way an adult daughter would her sick mother. Worst of all, it reminded Ren that she'd never had a daughter—only a son. A son she tried so hard not to think about. A son who'd driven her to this mountain by becoming something not unlike the woman stroking her neck.

Humiliation swelled in her, as did hate, shame, disgust, but she was too feverish to feel any of it with conviction. The water kept trickling, cool and lovely. Harker's hand stroked on.

Harker was talking now, small words in her ear.

I'm so glad you've decided to help us. Now we can help you.

She waved at the trees, and two soldiers pushed out of the foliage. One of them was carrying a first-aid kit, the other a large backpack.

See to her wound, ordered Harker, as she gently removed Ren's head from her lap and stood up. Give her medicine, anti-biotics—whatever she needs.

Harker stretched her arms wide and looked up at the sky. She exhaled, loudly, as if she'd arrived at the end of a long day or put down a heavy weight. Only then did she motion at her other soldiers, beckoning them forth from the trees. Six figures walked out. Four were young men in uniform, but the two others, walking between them, were of different ages. One was just a boy, while the other was older, with grey streaking his hair. This older man was limping, and a purple-yellow bruise was splashed across his face. The boy stayed close by his side, making sure he did not fall.

Ren only recognised them when they were almost close enough to touch. She tried to stand up, but the dizziness and the pain and the confusion swirled together to make her slip back down. Barlow was trying to smile at her, but the act of smiling was beyond him.

She wanted to scream. She wanted to vomit. But all she could do was lie there, ruined and weak, as Harker laughed. Her joy reverberated off the cliff and around the clearing in high peals, before she turned to her men.

See? I told you we wouldn't need them.

THEY LET HER rest. She sat on the ground, chewing on a muesli bar and sipping from a bottle of fizzing, bright-yellow liquid—water that one of the soldiers had infused with two vitamin tablets. She was given six pills, all different colours and shapes, which she swallowed without question.

Another soldier knelt to inspect her arm. He was perhaps the youngest of the group: pink-faced, beardless, polite.

Hello, he said in a quiet, hesitant voice. My name is Daniel. I'm a medic.

She did not answer, did not look at him. He seemed to want to say something else, and there was an apologetic air to his presence. But he stayed silent, and after a moment he got to work, removing her bandage, washing the wound with water and iodine. Then he treated it with padding, some kind of cream, a fresh dressing.

Once the infection is cleared up it'll need stitches, he said. He looked Ren in the face as he spoke, making sure she understood.

She looked past him, didn't react. He opened his mouth to speak again, but decided against it. He stood and left her, and she continued to sit still and quiet. She didn't even try to talk to Barlow, who was sitting on the other side of the clearing and murmuring to his son, the bruise loud on his face. After half an hour Harker checked her watch and turned to Ren.

Time to go.

A soldier helped Ren to her feet. Her head swam as she was pulled upright, and her arm ached, but the pain was blunted. She walked to the path leading away from the cave, and continued to ignore Barlow and his son as she addressed their captors.

This way.

Harker and three of the soldiers, including the young medic, fell in step behind her. The others stayed by Barlow and his son. Ren didn't look at them, nor did she or Harker say anything. There was nothing worth saying.

During the rest, Ren had wondered if there was any point in helping the soldiers. She thought it unlikely they'd let her live, even if she delivered them a flock of rain herons. Harker would probably shoot her the moment they caught the bird. She'd have Barlow shot as well, and his boy. They'd leave, tell nobody about it, and nobody in the village would complain, lest more soldiers stomped into their lives.

But there was a chance they wouldn't. There was a chance all three of them would survive. Or just the boy: the boy was enough. This made her think of her son again, her furious son, shouting and shaking in the moments before he left her. She pushed him from her mind, focused again on the present. Even if she decided against helping the soldiers, would she be able to resist them? Harker had already broken her once. Ren had given in so easily, her head cradled in Harker's lap like a child's. Her conviction, which she had been so sure of, so quietly proud of—gone, for a drop of water.

She felt stronger now, but that strength wouldn't last, not if she took a stand against them. Harker would take it away; she would have so many ways of turning her, of twisting her, of slicing pieces off everything left of her. Ren realised that she wasn't that strong—maybe she never had been. The water, food, vitamins and medicine sloshed inside her shrunken stomach. She walked on.

It had been so many years since she'd journeyed to the bird's tarn, and even then she'd been tired, and it had been dark—she probably couldn't have found her way there the day after her first trip, let alone now, decades later and half-delirious. Yet, as she walked, making for the edge of the forest where she knew the trees gave way to open slopes, things started feeling familiar—certain patterns in the treescape, the shape of the cliffs above. When they reached the forest's end she saw a steep, flat plain, devoid of the usual rubble and rocks, sloping upwards to a single peak. Again she felt a burn of familiarity.

Harker pointed at the dark heights.

Up there?

Ren leaned into her knees.

Yes.

They began the ascent. With no trees to provide cover they were exposed to the wind, which buffeted them from the south, hitting them in huge, unpredictable gusts, knocking even Harker off balance. Ren soon ran out of lungs, and kept needing to stop. Nobody tried to hurry her. After every such break one of the soldiers would grip her wrist and pull her to her feet. Another would hand her a water bottle or piece of hard, waxy chocolate. They were gentle with her, and she hated them, even the young medic who'd patched up her arm.

They climbed on, and the effects of the medicine began to wear off. Exhaustion reappeared in Ren's legs, her back, her breaths. The pain and nausea returned. Her eyes were closed more than they were open, and it was only the soft hands of the soldiers, who had begun more or less shovelling her uphill, that kept her going. That, and the thought of Barlow walking down the mountain with his son.

Despite her déjà vu, she still wasn't sure they were going the right way—not until, as if appearing from behind a bank of fog, a flat, cracked wall of rock loomed before them. She wondered how she'd managed to find it; the odds must have been remarkable; but there it was, huge, high, dark. She must have made a noise, because the soldiers all turned to stare at her. She pointed at the jagged aperture.

There. We go through there.

Harker nodded. She was the first to bend her body into the contours of the rock and disappear. A soldier followed her, then another. The last was Daniel, the young medic, who laid a soft hand between Ren's shoulders and guided her forward.

Before she stepped inside she drew in a long, cold lungful of air. The sun was just beginning to set, and she wanted everything to be over. There, on the slope, with the wind on her skin, the trees below her and the falling, glowing sun above. But the soldier pushed again, and with great difficulty she negotiated her way through the rock. Emerging into the crevasse on the other side felt just as it had all those decades earlier—like coming up for air after a deep dive. It was just as Ren remembered: the tight rock scraping her shins and elbows, the sky clear above, the claustrophobic cling of the walls.

She could hear the soldiers' breaths growing shallow. They were staring upwards, straining their necks at the high cliffs. Only Harker was moving forward along the path. They wriggled on after her, and in what seemed a short amount of time—short to Ren, although time and a feeling of its passing were no longer clear to her—they reached the grand amphitheatre.

The tarn lay still and mirror-like, just as it had when she'd first seen it. Moss still carpeted the grotto floor, green rocks still humped at the tarn's edge, and the ancient, gnarled tree still stood on the opposite side of the water. The soldiers spread out, taking in the scene, the strangeness of it, the glory of the approaching night, the ocean of forest that spread out from the far cliff. Harker turned to Ren.

It lives here?

Ren nodded. The exhaustion had hooked her now, tight and hard, and the waking hallucinations had returned. Faces, shapes, memories: all there, all blurring. She slumped to the edge of the tarn. This time nobody helped her.

When does it return?

I don't know.

Ren focused on the greenness of the moss, at her reflection in the water.

When it wants to.

Harker said something to one of the soldiers, who grasped Ren under the arms and dragged her backwards, propping her against the cliff, halfway back into the crevasse they'd come through. They stopped talking to her after that. She was left to watch as Harker prowled around the pond, fiddling with her ponytail, flexing her fingers, before she ordered the soldiers to position themselves around the tarn. They each crouched down behind a rock, hiding themselves as much as possible. Harker moved to a slender hollow in the cliff, right behind the tree.

They waited. Ren was dozing now, sliding in and out of consciousness. Scenes of heat and rain flashed through her. She could have been kinder, she thought. She should have been less cold, should have cultivated better, deeper relationships. Other people—she should have poured more energy into helping other people. What would they say about her, those people back in the city, those that were left? That she was hard. Yes. They'd say she was hard as granite. That they didn't really know her. Maybe they'd say she was a good mother. Maybe they'd say nothing at all—maybe most of them hadn't even noticed when she left. Throbs and flashes of sickness kept washing through her, on great blood-borne waves, right up until the moment she saw, for the second time in her life, a bird made of water.

It erupted from the tarn in smooth, splashless flight, heading up in a straight leap to hover effortlessly in the air before alighting on a low branch of the tree. It buried its beak in a wing, flicking water back and forth in neat, sure dips. It looked just as Ren remembered, or thought she remembered: the same marvellous grace, the same rain-smeared transparency. It sat there, its watery body shimmering and glistening, unaware of Ren or Harker or the soldiers.

Despite the horror of her situation, Ren still felt a sense of wide-eyed awe at what she was seeing. The bird took her out of herself. She watched it preen, fastidious and thorough. She strained to keep her eyes open, fighting the liquid springing from their corner; she concentrated on staying conscious.

It was only when Harker had moved completely out of her cover that Ren saw her noiselessly inching forward. In her hands she clutched a wide, dark cloth. It was glossy black, treated with oil or tar. As she watched Harker move, Ren realised how much she didn't want to let her win. She wanted the bird to stay free, but mostly she wanted Harker to lose, to be thwarted. To feel pain.

Harker had made it to within two metres of the tree when Ren, thinking not of Barlow or the boy or herself or her son or of anything but her anger, shouted. She shouted as loud as her broken body could manage. The bird's neck snapped upwards, needled her with a swirling, daggering eye; Harker leapt, holding the cloth high and wide.

Before Ren could see the result, one of the soldiers appeared in front of her. It was the young medic—Daniel. He loomed close and high above her, and there was sadness on his clean skin, on his round face. His pale eyes were dragged by heavy sorrow, which intensified into regret, even as he swung the butt of his rifle into her jaw.

A crack filled Ren's ears, and she slammed into the ground. Hollowness welled up inside her. Black fields. As she flickered out of consciousness, she thought she could hear screaming.

SHE SWAM THROUGH heavy darkness. No dreams. No visions. Just the absence of light and the feeling of weightlessness, punctuated by a rolling rhythm of bumps.

Eventually, Ren opened her eyes. She was lying on the ground by the entrance to her cave. Her jaw was aching, and so was the rest of her head: a full-skull throb that pulsed at her eyes, which felt too big for their sockets. Her mind churned with colours and broken images.

She eased into a sitting position. The sun was up, but not high. Long spears of light were strafing across the clearing.

The soldiers were sitting around her fire pit. They were speaking to each other in low voices, their mouths and eyes pointed at the ground. A few metres away she could see Barlow and his son, prone, their heads propped up against a log. For a moment she thought they were dead, but then she saw the rise and fall of Barlow's chest. Relief swam down from her neck to her knees.

She looked around the clearing, past the soldiers, and saw a large box-like object sitting near the path. A black piece of canvas had been thrown over it. Beyond it sat Harker, cross-legged on the ground, facing the trees. Her back was straight, her ponytail high. Something was wrong with her, Ren could tell: a certain rigidity to her posture, a stiffness in her arms, the speed at which her shoulders moved with each breath. It made Ren nervous—this ever-calm, ever-composed young officer, sitting so fiercely, with so much intent.

Ren remembered the screams.

She stood up. None of the soldiers noticed. She walked forward, feeling light, strange, a narrow and woozy version

70

of herself. The pain in her arm was distant again—more like the knowledge of pain than a sensation of it. She stepped towards the canvas-covered box, feeling the wind on her skin, smelling the resin in the air. Still the soldiers did not notice her.

When Ren reached the box she knelt before it. A noise was shuddering out from behind the stiff cloth—a low, pattering noise, like light rain. At first Ren thought it was some kind of engine, but then she heard the inconsistencies in it, a pattern of slight changes in tone. Up and down, high and low. Inhalations and exhalations in the downpour.

She reached forward to grasp the edge of the canvas. The oil-stiff fabric bent beneath her fingers, and the rain-breath behind the curtain quickened. As it did, something struck her chest with enough force to throw her onto her back. Falling, she heard a high, familiar scream.

Her head smacked against the dirt. She scrambled up onto her elbows, disoriented. Harker was above her. One of her legs was half-raised, and on her face, in her stance, in her pumping chest and even shimmering in the air around her was a pure bloom of rage. It writhed across her features, baring her teeth, flaring her nostrils, sapping her skin pale and widening her eye.

It wasn't just fury that was distorting her face; a river of blood had flowed and dried down her right cheek in a rusty, flaking trail. Above it was only a deep echo of flesh. The empty socket glowed with red rawness. Harker's lips were moving, but she wasn't speaking. Her skin swam with hues of pink, red, purple.

Ren was sure she'd reached the moment of her death, that Harker would kill her as soon as she decided on a method. And she might have, if it hadn't been for Barlow, who, awakened by Harker's scream, had stood up and slowly walked over to stand by Ren.

Please. She didn't mean anything.

Harker ignored him. The soldiers had looked up but not moved, not even the one named Daniel, the one who'd hit her with his rifle. Still Harker stared down at Ren; still her body twitched with feverous rage.

Barlow continued: I'll take her away. We'll go. You've got what you came for.

He moved forward, arms splayed in front of him, conciliatory and calm, and finally he snagged Harker's attention. She dragged her eye up from Ren to Barlow, before taking a quick step towards him and slashing a leg forward in a vicious, whipping strike, buckling his knees, toppling him. She began screaming at him—more high, wordless howls. It seemed certain that she'd fall upon him, rip at his body with teeth and nails.

Even in this mania, her grace was still present. On she screamed, her whole body rigid, shaking. Barlow's son had woken up and run forward, but a soldier had caught him by the neck and was holding him high in the air, little arms pinned tight, as screams poured out of his young body, mingling with Harker's.

Ren watched it happen. She would have done something. She would have stopped it all. But she couldn't, and she knew it, so she did the only thing that occurred to her. She crawled back to the box and thrust a hand beneath the canvas. She felt cold, hard rods—metal bars. A cage. She ran her palm over each bar, circling the structure until she found a latch. The sound from within grew into a pelting crash of water. Her fingers fidgeted with the mechanism.

A loud click chimed from beneath her fingers. The door to the cage creaked beneath the pressure of her hand, and the sound of rain reached a storming crescendo—the sound of breaking banks and coming floods.

Harker stopped screaming. She turned to the cage as Barlow flinched, as his son sobbed, as Ren tugged on the metal. A crack of thunder joined the storm. The door was halfway open, pushing against the canvas, when Harker, suddenly calm again—as if the shock of seeing the cage being opened had snapped her back into her trained state of tranquillity—pulled her pistol from its holster, aimed it at Ren and fired in one fluid, graceful movement.

The bullet tore into the base of Ren's throat. Her body crashed into the cage, slamming the door shut. Ravens burst from the trees around the clearing, their rasps long and loud. The sound of rain disappeared. The stream gurgled. The wind blew, thick with the scent of pine.

PART 2

YEARS EARLIER, ON the country's south coast, a small port suffered an uncommonly brutal winter. It was always cold in the port, but this winter was worse than any other in living memory. Hail filled the wind; ice glazed the streets. The gardens were scraped rough and gorgeous by frost. People stitched themselves into woollen cocoons. Blood slowed. Skin tore. Despite the cold, it never snowed.

Even in milder weather, it didn't make much sense to live there. The people who did claimed that they stayed for the port's sharp beauty. It was surrounded by long squeaky beaches of cloud-white sand, so pure that visitors often thought the grains were snowflakes. Huge humps of grey-pink granite rose behind the beaches, sparkling in the thin light, rolling into large hills and small mountains. Gnarled trees were scattered in the gullies between the rocks, bent to wild angles by the ceaseless attention of the wind.

Beyond the granite and sand was the dark sea, slashed white by the wind, and in the midst of all these colours and textures and elements, perched between rock and sand and water, was the port's town. Its buildings were small, built with bleached wood and cement. Smoke leaked from chimneys at all hours, all year. Pale piers pushed out into the ocean, tethering boats, gathering salt. There was no arguing that the place was beautiful; but beauty could not fill stomachs or clothe backs.

The real reason people lived at the port was a particular resource, found nowhere else. It wasn't the snow-bright sand or the iron-tough trees. It wasn't the nutrient-rich seaweed that clumped on the shore. It wasn't the muscle of the wind, and it wasn't the glint of the granite (which, although striking, was impossible to mason and largely worthless). The jewel of the port was something not easily seen—a slippering, shimmering treasure that only the port people knew how to find.

TWO YEARS BEFORE that harsh winter, a boat sped away from the port's blinking shore. On it was a girl named Zoe. She had never been to sea before, and the lurch of the water was sending rubber into her legs. Her messy red-brown hair whipped free from the band holding it back and slapped at her eyes. Towards the prow, her aunt pushed the throttle. The boat raised its nose and picked up speed. Zoe collapsed into a bench at the back, raised her collar to the cold. Her aunt stayed upright, teasing the wheel with a bent finger.

Zoe turned to face the town, watching it glint until it was no longer discernible. The sea around them grew darker than the blue-green tides she was used to. Soon the waves stopped breaking, the white lick of their caps replaced by rippled, changeable humps. Above them the sky was thickening with clouds. She huddled into her jacket.

After an hour her aunt pulled up the throttle, bringing the engine to silence and slowing the boat in a sudden wash of foam.

This should do.

She pulled a large net from a compartment on the side of the boat, and laid it on the floor. Then she retrieved some plastic trays from the boat's tiny cabin. She turned to her niece, her face serious.

You know what we're doing?

Zoe nodded.

You know how it's done? Has anyone told you?

Zoe shook her head.

Good.

Her aunt looked out at the water.

This time you'll watch. Just watch. Listen. And one day you can do it yourself, if you decide you want to. If you're willing to pay the price.

She began rolling up one sleeve of her padded jacket.

When the sleeve passed her elbow she moved to the edge of the boat.

Watch.

Zoe followed her. Her aunt's proximity to the water made her nervous, because she knew her aunt could not swim—none of the older people from the port could. Younger generations like Zoe's had been taught, but most people over thirty had never learned.

But this first fear of Zoe's disappeared when she saw the small curved knife her aunt pulled from a pocket in her trousers. She lifted it to the rough skin of her exposed forearm. Zoe's thoughts of currents and water temperatures disappeared as she looked at the knife, her aunt's arm, the scars on her skin.

She had seen them before. Their pale corrugations had winked and shone as her aunt cooked, washed dishes, fixed furniture. Zoe had assumed that little white scars were something all adults wore on the fleshy parts of their arms. They did not seem to trouble her aunt, so they did not trouble Zoe, not even when she saw the fresh bandages, the scarlet flare of the newest additions to her aunt's collection. But now, seeing the blade hover above her aunt's skin, a rush of realisation crashed through her.

Watch, her aunt repeated. In a slow, clean swoop the knife arced down, pressing into the skin before it broke and gave way, splitting open millimetres from a blue-purple vein. Blood sprang, but not in a gush or torrent like Zoe had feared. It leaked in a rich, even stream down her aunt's arm, which she had moved to hang over the side of the boat. The blood collected on the underside of her hand in a ponderous dollop before it fell through the cold air, carried sideways by the wind until it hit the sea.

Keep watching.

The blood drizzled into the navy. Her aunt's face showed no pain. Zoe felt sick, and scared, and somehow fouled, as if she was witnessing a circus trick gone horribly wrong—an elephant snapping a tusk, an acrobat garrotting himself on a wire.

Her aunt stayed still.

Only human blood works, she said finally. Other kinds have been tried. Nothing does the trick. Pig blood goes closest, but it doesn't get the same results. Makes them go all jangled and skittish. Hard to control.

Zoe stared at the waft of blood, her throat slick with bile. When the cloud had spread into the size of a quilt her aunt lifted her arm and wrapped a length of gauze around the wound.

Now we wait.

Zoe swallowed.

What happens? What do they do?

Her aunt nursed her arm and watched the water. Zoe stared at her, and felt herself grow colder, and did not watch the slopping sea until her aunt finally raised a hand and pointed at the waves.

They do that.

Zoe whipped her gaze to the bloodied sea. She saw only dark water and her aunt's drifting blood. But she heard a splash, from somewhere out of her eyeline. She moved closer to the side of the boat, and saw the water break. Something long and languid emerged from the sea. More shapes rose, strange and rubbery, pink-white against the navy, waving lazily in the air. Zoe watched. She did not blink, did not exhale: not until the owner of these tendrils floated up to the surface in the centre of the blood cloud.

The squid's wide violet hood was a metre long and half as wide at its blunt base. It tapered upwards, past the enormous yellow orbs that were its eyes, ending in a neat arrowed point of flesh. At least a dozen tentacles swam away from the body, working through the water, pushing small tides towards an opening in the hood that Zoe soon recognised as a beaked mouth, clacking at the reddened waves.

Her aunt touched Zoe's shoulder.

Wait a minute.

The beast drank, shovelling at the blood-water until almost all the crimson colour had vanished. Then it stopped. Its body bobbed upwards to float on the surface, and its huge yellow eyes dimmed behind a cloudy membrane.

Zoe turned to her aunt, panicking.

Is it dead?

No. Just resting.

Her aunt turned around, bent into the boat.

Just the way we want it.

When she straightened she was holding the net. She extended her arms, loosened it with a few shakes, then hefted it to the height of her chin.

I hope you're still watching, she said, before tossing it

overboard, where it spread in a wide dish above the comatose creature. When it landed Zoe waited for the beast to stir, but it didn't. The net draped gently over its body, small grey sinkers dropping the edges beneath its hood. Her aunt began reeling it in, hand over hand, and still the squid did not move. Its eyes remained clouded, its body listless, even as her aunt hauled it into the boat, grunting, heaving, sweating in the cold air.

Fill a bucket with water.

Zoe did as she was told, leaning over the side of the boat, wincing at the sea's bite on her hands. Bucket full, she turned back to see her aunt removing the net from the squid's body. She put it aside, then slid one of the plastic trays to lie at the base of the hood, right beneath the beak. Still the beast dozed, unaware that it had shifted worlds.

Her aunt pointed at the squid.

Pour some of that water on it. Use a cup.

Zoe filled a mug from the bucket and splashed it onto the fleshy hood. Her aunt frowned.

Slower. But keep it up. Keep it steady.

Zoe began trickling the water in a thin stream, and her aunt moved to kneel before the beaked maw.

I've been telling you to watch me all day, but this part is the most important thing you need to see.

She reached for her bandage, pulled it carefully upwards until the gash was revealed. Blood began to ooze down her arm again. She lifted her wrist and knelt before the beast, her knees inches from its beak. She wriggled, positioning herself for an act Zoe could not anticipate. When it came, it was simple: her aunt leaned into the squid's maw and raised her hand high. Blood ran down her skin and collected on the point of her elbow in a thick droplet. She manoeuvred her arm, aiming for something Zoe could not see, until she'd found her target. With a wriggle of her wrist the droplet fell. The orb of blood descended, round and bright, and landed on a small white gland that sat just above the bony beak.

The clouds misted away from the squid's great eyes. Zoe sucked in a breath and paused her pouring. Her aunt's face flashed up at her.

Don't stop. We're nearly done.

The golden eyes rolled, rising suns, and her aunt stood up, re-bandaging her wound.

A sudden wave of iridescence flashed across the creature's body, flickering from the point of the hood to the end of the slack tentacles. Zoe leapt backwards. Her aunt grinned as waves of colour began dancing across the squid. Its pale-purple form began hosting splashes of gold, bursts of blueness, vivid greens and reds and blues that swirled and danced across the unsquirming flesh.

Get ready, murmured her aunt, and as she said it Zoe saw the final act: a thick stream of blue-black liquid shot out from somewhere near the squid's beak, landing in the waiting tray. Her aunt shifted her stance as more of this substance gushed out. Enough came to fill the tray, and she quickly swapped it out for a second. When this was half-full, the stream thinned. The shifting colours on the squid's body began to slow, to shine less sharply. When the dark liquid had decreased to a trickle the creature settled back into its former shade of pale purple. And when no more liquid flowed, her aunt stood.

Quick. We need to get it back into the water.

They did not use the net this time. Zoe followed her aunt's lead in handling the squid gently, almost tenderly. The flesh was slimy and heavy under her hands. Together they lifted it over the edge of the boat and dipped it tentacles-first into the sea. They held it there, letting it find its strength and bearings. When it began to wriggle against them her aunt loosened her grip.

It's time. Let go.

Zoe did as she was told. The beast hung in the water for a moment, as if paused in thought, before gathering its appendages around its eyes and propelling itself downwards, pushing fast into the brine.

It was gone. Zoe blinked. She rubbed at her head. She was filled with confusion and astonishment and an ache of loss at the disappearance of the creature. She wanted it to come back, although she wasn't sure why. She turned around to see her aunt carefully decanting one of the trays into a large glass container, not spilling a drop. When her aunt was finished she straightened up, saw Zoe watching her, and let out a sudden burst of laughter. It rang loud, a chime that raced across the sea's chop before she spoke again.

Not so hard, was it?

She pointed at her bandaged arm, at the bottle containing their blue-black haul.

Blood for ink. A simple trade.

They decanted the second tray, then gunned back to port. The time passed strangely for Zoe, as if elasticised by her tiredness. Eventually she saw winking lights on the horizon, and realised it was the sun reflecting off the white sand and the granite hills surrounding the town. She watched them grow in size and brightness until a thin curtain of rain began to fall, swamping it all in grey.

THE INK WAS sold to people from the north, then churned, vaporised, and used to make perfectly antiperspirant deodorant that rendered pores sweatless and odourless for up to three days. It was added to sauces and stews to create a rich, meaty-fishy flavour, or mixed with vegetable gum and powdered horse hooves into a paste that was sold as industrial-grade engineering glue. It was greased onto engines to provide unusually long-lasting lubrication, and it was brewed into a black wine that hit the tongue like a sweet ocean breeze. But it was most commonly used as dye.

When mixed with other colours of dye (or paint or chalk or lesser inks) it vastly enhanced the qualities of that colour, in the same way that salt brings out depth of flavour in food. Adding it to a matte red would bring out a bright pop of open-vein crimson, while mixing it with a basic purple would create violent blinks of violet. It lent a soft, mossy texture to an average dark green, and a navy depth to dark blue that was so strong it brought about the smell of the sea. White shone brighter; orange shimmered like a sunset. Pale blue became so skylike it made one forget about the existence of clouds.

ZOE KEPT GOING out with her aunt, although her aunt did all the bleeding. She itched to wear scars of her own, to draw the squid with her blood, but her aunt would not allow it.

When you're older, she'd say. Your mother would kill me if I let you open a vein at your age.

Then she would laugh, because Zoe's mother was dead. Her aunt didn't find that funny—she laughed because she laughed at everything. It was the only response she was capable of, regardless of the situation. She laughed at jokes and television, but she also laughed at food and trees and weather reports. Breakfast made her laugh, as did rain, splinters and trousers. She laughed at good fortune and horror. The more tense or difficult the circumstances, the wilder she laughed. When she learned that her sister—Zoe's mother—had died, she screamed, bit her cheek and cackled, spraying blood from her mouth across a tiled floor.

Zoe's aunt's laughter was as common as wind and as regular as the tides. So when her aunt wouldn't let her bleed, Zoe was not hurt by the laughs that came with the refusal. And although she chafed at the decision, she obeyed her aunt. Zoe had no father—the man had been a trader who docked at the port for a night and never returned—and her mother had died when she was four. Her aunt was the whole of her world. To be like her, to bleed like her—that was all Zoe wanted. When she thought of the scars she would own, the beasts she would summon, her face would heat and her mind would swell and shake. She was willing to be patient.

They went on short, early morning ink trips before school, at an hour where the sun had not yet lit a glow in the granite hills. On weekends they took longer trips, ones that resulted in huge hauls of ink and the occasional purchase of a blood transfusion for her aunt. At school Zoe used a blunt biro to draw blue premonitions into her elbows. Out at sea she watched the knife slide open her aunt's salted skin. She studied the flow of blood, how long it took for squid to appear, how long for them to gorge themselves senseless.

The sea wind cut her sharp and hard. Bright-dark ink slopped their bottles full. For two years Zoe rode the boat and pulled the nets, her skin full of hunger, her ears full of laughter. Then the uncommonly cold winter hit.

As if borne on the weather's cruelty, the northerner came to the port.

HE HAD SHORT black hair and a face the colour of sour milk. His size and features were all unremarkable, and his clothes were the kind one would usually see in the north: denim trousers, thin shirts, jackets full of buttons. He didn't wear any small, expensive hats, but he seemed like the sort of man who would. There was nothing about him that suggested danger. He was just a visitor, and he was paid little heed.

He came to the port at the start of winter. Like most visitors, he arrived on a boat. The town was accessible by a highway, but it meandered circuitously through the swamps and mountains that lay between the port and the north of the country, so it was far quicker to come via the sea. The northerner's boat was an old, once-sleek speedboat, the sort used for towing water skis or hosting on-water picnics. Nobody at the port liked the look of it. It was a leisure boat, unsuited to their tastes, their work, this part of the country. When they met the owner, their impression did not improve, although that had nothing to do with his appearance or foreignness.

The day he arrived he steered his speedboat into the dock, tethered it to a salted pylon, disembarked and strode down the pier. He smiled at the few people he saw, but did not stop to speak. He walked a slow lap of the town, threading through the small network of cobbled streets and alleys, before entering a large pub that sat on the waterfront, overlooking the harbour.

Inside, his attention was snared by a large painting that dominated the rear wall of the room. It was a simple image—a dark, empty ocean meeting a clear horizon. But there was something in this painting that was impossible to look away from—a depth in the colours and textures that the northerner had never seen before. The murk of the sea was salty and wet to stare at, and looking at the point where the water met the pale, cloudless sky filled him with a sense of dread, as if dry land would forever be out of reach. He shivered in the warm room. It was the first time he'd seen an artwork laced with ink, although he didn't know it at the time.

Eventually he dragged his eyes from the painting and ordered a beer, which he sipped over the course of the evening, letting the golden tide lap at his lip as the boats came into the dock, as the pub filled with patrons, as the seabirds called through the windows, as the sun dropped and disappeared.

When the room heaved with people he lifted his beer and began moving around the room, although he didn't talk to anyone; he just wandered, studying the painting, as well as the shark jaws and nautical apparel on the walls, pretending he wasn't listening to what the port people were saying to each other. None of them were fooled. They had seen out-of-towners like him before—ones who had acted the same way, with the same intentions. So they kept drinking, and kept speaking about everything they would usually speak about in public, and waited for his questions to come.

When they did, the pub was about to close. The northerner was nearing the bottom of his beer, while most of the locals were finishing their sixth or seventh. As the barman rang his bell, the stranger downed his watery dregs, slid onto a stool by a group of young men and addressed them.

I'm sorry to interrupt, but I was wondering if you knew where I might get my hands on some south-sea ink?

The young men, red-cheeked, loose-limbed, all nodded.

One of them acted as spokesman.

Us. Meet us here tomorrow. Bring cash.

Thanks, but what I meant was: where can I get it myself?

Yourself?

Yes. Myself.

With your own hands?

Yes, that's it.

The young man drenched his throat with the rest of his beer. You said south-sea ink, right?

Yes. South-sea ink.

Ah. That's the problem. It doesn't exist.

Pardon?

It's a trick. One we play on northerners. It's not real.

He left. The door swung shut behind him. The other young men drained their pints and, without acknowledging the northerner, followed their companion into the lightless street. The northerner turned around, a smile drawn onto his lips, and looked for someone else to speak to. But the rest of the patrons were also leaving. Within a minute the northerner was standing alone at the bar, trying to make eye contact with departing drinkers who would not look at his face, even as their shoulders bumped his chest. Behind him, the publican coughed. A light was dimmed. The northerner left, and slept under mounds of blankets in the cabinless prow of his speedboat.

The following night he returned to the pub, bought another beer. This time he downed it quickly, ordered another, and began speaking to anyone who would turn his way. His questions were similar to the one he'd posed to the young man the night before—about the ink, where he could get some, how it was collected. Earnestness shone in his face, an enthusiasm that the port people found as unseemly as his questions.

Most of them ignored him, but some found the manners to answer. One bearded seafarer told him that he was in the wrong town, that the ink came from a different port. Another repeated the young man's claim from the night before about the ink being a trick, while another swore to him that it was a myth, like a unicorn or a rain heron. One woman told him that the ink was actually inside us all, like love or kindness or friendship. At least three people said they'd never heard of south-sea ink, and five or six made confused, miming signs, as if they did not understand the language he spoke.

An hour passed, then another, and still the northerner received answers that were cryptic at best, insulting at worst. He drank three more beers, then another. The earnestness in his face wobbled into exasperation, then annoyance, and finally into desperation. When that happened—when a look of ragged despair settled onto his off-white features—he drained his sixth beer, turned to face the room, pushed his back against the bar and began speaking in a loud, faltering voice.

Excuse me. Excuse me. I'm sorry to interrupt your evening. I won't take up much of your time.

Then, in sentences that at first were short but became longer, he began taking up their time. He understood why they didn't want to tell him about the ink, he said. He knew that others like him had come to the port seeking quick fortunes, to plunder the town's resource in harsh, destructive ways. But he was not like that, he assured them. That was not his aim. He wanted to help them. He had plans to build a sustainable fishery that produced greater yields of ink, yields that would benefit them all. Sensible expansions; larger contracts with trusted wholesalers; long-term security for their industry. In these times of strife and uncertainty, he said, we need to be prepared for change. He wanted to walk with them into the future, he said, hand in hand, or something to that effect. By then his face and neck were red, and sweat was popping through his skin. After the bit about walking hand in hand, he stopped talking. He looked around the room, his face glowing with exertion and passion.

The patrons had shown him respect by listening. They hadn't muttered or stared into their beer. But as soon as he stopped speaking they turned to each other, resumed their drinking and their conversations, and made no sign of having heard his speech, or having noticed him at all. He waited another moment, still expectant, but as the chatter built and the room kept ignoring him, he realised he had failed. The talk swelled louder as he pushed away from the bar. Nobody spoke to him. Nobody looked at him. There was no sign that his existence had been noted—no sign but for a peculiar sound ringing out above the chatter.

It was a loud, gleeful sound, rich in timbre and full of humour. A torrent of laughter, built with huge exhalations that rolled over the room, coming from somewhere near the end of the bar. The northerner had already begun to leave, but on his way out, his despair replaced by sorrow, he pinpointed the source of the noise.

It was Zoe's aunt. The other drinkers were still pretending he didn't exist, but she was staring straight at him as she slapped at the bar, her chest, her knees. Beer splashed from her lips as she laughed, and anyone who looked at the northerner would have seen his soul plunge. Before the night swallowed him, they locked wet eyes—hers leaking mirth, his streaming shame.

IT WAS AROUND this time that the severity of the weather began to be commented on. The season was only just beginning, but the air already held the deep chill of midwinter, a cold that dried eyes and sprang nosebleeds. Winter mornings were usually still, with angry gusts building in the afternoon. But the days were beginning with fat bursts of wind, thumping at windows, ripping up conversations, slapping the ocean and curdling its waves. Frost was expected in the mornings, but at this time of year it would usually melt soon after sunrise. Instead it was lingering, even when unhidden by shadow, staying slick and hard until lunchtime. The port people shivered, complained, swung their numb arms, and when they saw the northerner they wondered if he knew how cruel the days were being, if he had any idea what he'd walked into.

If he did, he gave no sign. He was regularly seen walking around the docks at first light, his eyes locked on the water or clouds as if deep in thought. He seemed to have recovered from his embarrassment at the pub, although he'd stopped asking questions. He didn't speak to the port people as they went about their work, didn't even look at them, didn't respond to Zoe's aunt's giggles as the pair strode past him towards their boat. They and the other harvesters motored out to sea, and the northerner spent his day strolling through town, failing to climb the granite hills, sleeping in the cold, unprotected cabin of his speedboat. But when the ink boats returned to the dock he was always back on the pier, wandering—in a manner obviously intended to appear aimless—in vague circles that led him closer and closer towards the docking boats.

Zoe and her aunt weren't the only ones who noticed him

peering nonchalantly at their decks. But like the other harvesters they ignored him, even as he, pretending he'd seen something in the water by their boat, used a little disposable camera to take photos of the ink they carried ashore.

Over the next week Zoe, her aunt and the other harvesters continued to ignore him. They ignored his wan smiles and polite nods every time they passed him in the street. They ignored the way he sat on the end of the dock sketching pictures of their boats and nets and the equipment on their decks. They ignored his offers of help in unloading their cargo, and they ignored the way he'd shadow them as they spoke to wholesalers.

The only time his presence was difficult to ignore was at the end of the week, when he climbed into his speedboat at dawn and followed one of the ink boats out to the squid grounds. The harvester he'd followed dropped his anchor, pulled out a thermos and spent the day at sea drinking tea, reading a paperback and eating sandwiches, before returning at dusk, followed again by the northerner's speedboat, which had been floating by his side all day. At the dock he explained what had happened to five or six other harvesters, who each poured a few fingers of fresh ink from their own bottles into his empty one.

When the bottle was half-full the northerner had just made it back to port. As he exited his speedboat the harvester he'd followed approached him, waving the bottle. The northerner looked confused, although this confusion did not stay long. It was wiped away by the harvester's free hand, which curled into a fist and slammed into his jaw.

The northerner's legs were already wobbly from the day on the water; at the connection of the punch they gave way, surrendering his body to the hardness of the pier. At the meaty thud of flesh on timber, the harvester shoved his fist into his pocket and walked away, a tuneless whistle pushing through his lips. The other harvesters secured their boats, collected their ink, moved towards the lights of the town.

Only Zoe, too young to fully commit to this performance, paid the northerner any attention. Only she saw the bloody phlegm he spat through the slats in the pier, saw it hit the water and mingle with the wash of a wave. Only she heard the sobs, harsh and heavy, that came from him. Only Zoe saw the pistol he pulled from the back of his belt to hold flat against the wood, pointed at nothing and no one, as his sobs broke apart.

THE NORTHERNER CAME to their house a few days later. It was a weekday evening, an hour after dinner. Winter's grip was tightening: the wind outside was thick with ice. Zoe's aunt let him in, chuckling as he shook and shivered.

As he sat at the table Zoe thought of the gun, and her pulse leapt, her breaths halted. They didn't start again until her aunt spoke.

Tea?

He nodded.

Yes. Thank you. And thank you for allowing me the time to speak with you.

Who said anything about speaking? I just offered you tea.

She filled the kettle, fished around in the cupboards.

Yes. Well.

They waited for the kettle to boil. Zoe was sitting on their couch, a small two-seater that was pushed against the far wall of the little room that served as their kitchen, dining room and lounge. She had a book open on her lap, but had stopped reading. She stared at the page, letting the letters blur. Her aunt leaned against the sink, humming. The northerner looked at his blue hands.

When the kettle clicked off her aunt poured water into three cups and handed them out, before settling into the seat opposite their guest.

So, how can we help you?

The northerner cleared his throat and sat up straight, although he didn't make eye contact with either of them.

I would like to reiterate my thanks for your kindness and hospitality. I truly appreciate it.

Her aunt snorted. The northerner blinked, but did not stop.

I believe you were in the pub on the night I recently visited? The night I spoke?

Good pub, isn't it? Great steak.

Yes, I'm sure. He took a breath. Then you must have heard what I said. How I am here to help revitalise the south-sea ink industry. To modernise it. To help you all safeguard its future, to guarantee its supply.

Her aunt leaned back in her chair, still smiling.

Yes, I remember some of that. How interesting.

The northerner's eyes swung upwards as Zoe's aunt sipped.

You're interested?

I said it's interesting.

What is?

That you don't know anything about this industry—ink, did you say? I'm afraid I haven't heard of it—but you plan on, what was it you said? Revitalising it? Safeguarding it?

A chuckle slipped from her lips. The northerner did not flinch.

I have certain expertise in this area. In many areas of business.

I'm sure you do.

She sipped again, a long draw of liquid.

I can't be the first person you've come to for help. You've been here for over a week.

I've enquired with many of your colleagues and neighbours.

And what did they tell you?

I think you know what they said to me. Or have a good idea.

Maybe. But who can be sure?

The northerner leaned forward onto the table.

Who can be sure of anything around here?

Zoe's aunt kept sipping her tea.

No idea.

The northerner rubbed at his face. Some seconds dripped past. He pushed his chair back.

Well, this was worth a try.

He looked at Zoe.

What about you?

Zoe flinched.

Me?

He looked into her face, fixing her still.

I've seen you go out on the boat. Can you help me? Help me help you all?

His expression was forlorn. Zoe felt frost in her stomach. Her mind snapped open the image of him on the pier, flattened, gun in palm. But her aunt beamed, seeming to grow more teeth as she turned to face the couch.

Zo, love, any idea what he's on about?

Zoe gulped.

Nope. Then, in a flash of inspiration, she said: We catch fish.

Her aunt's laughter burst through her teeth.

We sure do!

She turned back to the northerner.

Do you want some? We've got a whole freezer of, ah, what do you call it, flounder? Haddock? We've got it all.

The northerner's expression turned even more morose, and he pulled his eyes back to his shoes. He seemed to be thinking of something to say when Zoe's aunt pressed him further.

You don't just want to upgrade some old boats, do you? There's more to it than that, isn't there?

He hesitated.

Yes.

You owe people money? You gamble?

It's really nobody else's business...

Or it's a family thing? You need cash, and this is the only way you can think of getting it? Sick wife? Sick kids? Dog? There are easier ways to make money, son.

His eyes snapped up, and Zoe saw the same anger in him that she'd seen when he'd been punched: anger heated by shame. His next words had an edge that was completely unlike his usual, conciliatory tone.

You don't know what's happening in the rest of the country, do you?

We've heard things.

You clearly haven't heard enough.

The rage stayed in his voice as he stood, turning to the door.

Zoe's aunt followed him.

Look. You seem like a nice guy. But it doesn't matter how nice you are, or even how desperate. You aren't going to find what you're looking for.

He pulled on his jacket, muttering under his breath.

She slurped at her tea.

I'm trying to be kind.

Some tea drew up her nose, and despite the gravitas she was trying to summon she snorted, spraying tea onto the table, which prompted a bray of laughter.

He paused at the door. His voice was quiet.

Why do you keep laughing at me?

Zoe wanted to say something. She wanted to jump from the couch to yell that it wasn't him, that her aunt laughed at everyone and everything, but before she could speak her aunt laughed again, a ruckus of hard humour, and then the night blinked, winter ran inside, the door slammed, and the northerner was gone.

IN THE WEEKS that followed the wind grew sharper, the days shorter, the frost thicker. The northerner let go of the cautious optimism he had brought with him. His speedboat remained moored at the pier, but the man himself wasn't often spotted. When he was, it was usually on the beaches, wandering in jagged lines, staring out at the grey roof of the sea. The port people kept ignoring him, but in a way that was now more condescending. When he walked past they would exaggerate the way they'd move out of his way, or they stared up at the sky with comical effect, as if a low-flying plane had just buzzed past. If he spoke they whistled loudly, where before they'd just pretended not to hear him. He became a defeated figure, in the way he moved and the way he was treated. Only Zoe was cautious around him. Only she had seen his gun, and only she had noticed the depth of his determination.

In the evenings he went to the pub near the water. He'd sit alone at a booth by the window, under the ink-enriched painting, watching the sky and sea darken, drinking beer, eating steak. He spoke to no one, and nobody approached him. After his third or fourth pint he would take out a pen and a stack of clean paper, and start writing what looked like letters. The first few pages would come out quickly, his pen running clean lines across the paper, but as the evenings wore on his pace would slow. Steak glugged his stomach; beer dragged his blood. He'd lift his pen from the page and hesitate, his face all frowns and grimaces. Eventually he'd lower the pen again, but usually to rewrite his previous sentence, or to strike out whole lines. New words became less common than corrections. As his frowns grew he kept signalling the publican, whenever his glass clinked empty. He drained beer after beer. He would abandon trying to write new pages and start going back through the first ones he'd filled, taking his ink to them with hot vigour, deleting lines, marking large crosses across whole paragraphs, whole pages. By the time the publican was ringing his bell the northerner had thrown his pen at the window, as if aiming at the ocean beyond the glass, and was screwing all his pages into tight-scrunched missiles. As he lurched to the door he tossed the balled paper onto the pub's fire. By this time he was staggering, but he never missed the flames. The last thing he burned was always the one piece of paper he hadn't attacked—an envelope he'd laid beside his pages the moment he'd begun writing. He would watch the yellow flames chew up the name and address he'd printed neatly on its face. Then he'd crash through the door, drunk, letterless, alone.

It seemed inevitable that he'd leave. On the mornings or afternoons Zoe saw him—often clambering awkwardly in or out of his speedboat—she found herself wishing that it was the last time. Part of this desire came from her memory of his gun, but mostly she felt sorry for him. She knew that her aunt was right, and that every day he stayed was prolonging his suffering. She'd never even witnessed his aborted attempts at writing letters in the pub. If she had, she might have begged him to leave. Each time she saw the blend of shame and sorrow in his features she felt her guts twinge. She felt bad for him, and she felt bad about herself, for she had played a role in his sorrow—she had denied him, had lied to him. On her inking mornings her aunt would tread the pier, chuckle at his boat, and Zoe would stare at her boots or hands, wishing he would leave.

One cold morning, the sun weak and heatless above them, she and her aunt walked to their boat and saw that his was gone. Zoe felt a tide of relief wash through her, but didn't say anything. She was surprised, however, to hear her aunt blow out a sigh. She looked up and saw that her aunt had stopped walking.

Thank god. He was a determined one.

Zoe looked at the patch of water where the speedboat had been moored. I thought he was all right.

Oh yeah, he was all right. A perfect gentleman.

We didn't need to be so mean.

Her aunt rubbed her head.

It's the only way, love.

That day was the first time Zoe's aunt let her bleed. She'd wanted her aunt to do the cutting, but she'd been told that she had to do it herself or she'd never learn how to do it properly. Pressing the knife to her skin had felt unnatural, almost sickening. The coldness of the metal felt like a burn, before she'd even made the cut. She looked at her aunt, who nodded. The swell was light, the waves rocking the boat with weak force. Zoe bit the blade into her skin. Pain bloomed. She sucked air through clenched teeth and dragged the point of the knife down, half a centimetre, so the blood would run. Then she held her arm over the water and watched her blood free itself down her wrist, through the air, into the salt. When a fair-sized pool of it had fallen her aunt said: Enough, Zo, good job, and tugged the back of her shirt. Zoe stepped backwards as her aunt wrapped a bandage around the wound.

This'll make a neat little scar. Your mother's first was just like it.

Blood left Zoe's wound and rushed to her face. She sat down, dizzy. She stayed in this state, high and loose, as the squid rose to take her offering. She watched as her aunt waited for it to bob, then netted it, dragged it aboard, positioned the tray near its mouth. Zoe only stood back up when her aunt beckoned her. She moved to stand above the beast's great filmy eye, raised her opened arm and removed the bandage. When she felt the trickle of blood collect at her elbow she aimed, as she'd seen her aunt aim so many times, at the puckered white gland by the squid's beak. The drop fell, straight and true, and landed in the centre of the gland, which took on a sudden squirm. The huge eye unfilmed, resuming its golden stare, and the hood began shifting colours in wondrous, flickering patterns. Red-green-blue-purple-orange-yellow-pink, and all shades and hues in between, until the ink began to flow. Laughter bubbled from her aunt, in time with the gush of ink.

Bottles full, they returned to the port. Zoe's arm hurt, but the tight-wrapped pressure of the bandage had dulled the pain. She welcomed the sensation: it reminded her of what she'd finally achieved. Her aunt hummed something like a tune as they motored along, and the ink slopped in the jars, and when the port came into view Zoe thought that its light had never blinked so bright. Never had the sea and sand felt so welcoming. Never had the granite shined with such pale power.

Her mood stayed high, the world shinier in her eyes than it ever had been, until they reached the dock. As they were unloading their boat she bumped into her aunt's back. She glanced up, wondering why they'd stopped moving. Then she saw what her aunt was staring at.

The northerner's yellow speedboat was back, moored in its usual spot. The northerner himself was standing on its small deck, beside four rusted oil drums. He was rummaging around, doing something Zoe couldn't figure out, but when he saw them watching him a smile shone across his face—a toothy, lip-stretched smile, although his eyes remained flat and hard. Then he dipped a hand into the closest drum. He kept smiling as he pushed his whole forearm down, and still he smiled as he slowly removed it, as if teasing what he was about to show them.

His arm emerged red—a bright liquid red, from hand to elbow. He held it out and let the blood drip from his fingers. Scarlet spattered on yellow paint. His laugh shot across the cold pier, long and loud, happy and cruel.

ONE MORNING SOON after, the port people woke to white flakes falling from the sky. It had never snowed at the port, but it could be nothing else. It was cold, after all, as cold as anyone could remember: maybe snow had finally reached them. They tumbled outside, their palms pointing up, waiting to feel the sky's softness on their skin. But nothing touched them. They stared at each other across the frosted streets. The space between them seemed full of snowflakes, wafting in the easy morning wind. They could all see it. But none of it collected on the ground, or the roofs, or their outstretched hands. In under a minute the air cleared; the snowflakes, or whatever they'd been, stopped falling.

The port people rubbed at their eyes, swung their necks, touched the ground. Did you see it? they asked each other. Did you feel it? Where'd it go? They all agreed that the snow had been there; they had all witnessed it; they couldn't all have seen the same illusion. But the evidence had fled. Later-waking citizens didn't believe them. The ones who'd seen the snowfall turned bitter and bewildered. Anger stirred in them before they remembered the northerner and his barrels of blood.

Nobody knew where he'd learned about it. All the active harvesters denied having told him, and those who had retired kept their faces stony and didn't bother answering. When Zoe was asked she shook her head and told the truth: that the only time she'd spoken to the northerner was when he'd come to her aunt's house. She was believed, but her answer brought no satisfaction. The port people were furious that an outsider had discovered their secret, and they were hungry for someone to blame and punish.

It doesn't matter, said Zoe's aunt, a few days after he'd returned. It's not human blood; it won't work; he doesn't know what he's doing.

Zoe believed her—it seemed impossible that the mild northerner would have access to that much human blood—but she also heard the sullen worry in her aunt's voice and she realised that, since the northerner had returned, she hadn't heard her aunt laugh.

The northerner was laughing all the time. He paraded his knowledge up and down the dock, waving bloody fingers at anyone he saw, beaming and chuckling and telling anyone within earshot: Don't worry. Everything is going to be all right. Now we can start modernising. Now we can gain security.

But despite his confidence, he soon proved Zoe's aunt right. As he stalked the piers he was still staring into boats, studying the harvesters' gear. When he finally did take his boat and barrels out he returned empty-handed, although his smile did not waver. Three more fruitless journeys followed, although when he returned after the third he was breathless, excited, and could hardly keep his experience to himself.

After his fifth trip with the blood—on a grey day fat with wind and ice, the coldest day of the season so far—he returned to the dock late. The other inkers were already at home or the pub. The ones who were drinking noticed his return when they saw him through the pub windows, walking slowly down the pier, pushing into the wind. They turned back to their pints, and paid him no more attention until he had reached the town, when those glancing through the glass saw that he was dragging something along the cobbles. It was freezing outside, and nobody could be bothered to investigate until the northerner began shouting. Over the hubbub of the pub, these shouts pierced the windows and could not be ignored. Furious, triumphant, they grew louder and stranger, until the drinking inkers crashed down their glasses, abandoned the fire and trudged out into the winter's teeth.

They found the northerner in the middle of the street. Fog heaved from his lungs, frost hoared his buttons and wounds covered his skin. Scratches, bruises, cuts—he looked like he'd been in a road accident. His hands were the worst. They had been flayed, as if he'd been whipped or slashed, with skin hanging in strips from his fingers and the rent webbing between them. One thumb was shorn of its nail. Ice had filmed over the exposed meat. But despite these injuries he was still smiling, in the same manner he had ever since he'd returned with the barrels. Behind him was the misshapen, colourless hulk of a dead squid.

It had left a smear of mucous slime on the cobblestones it had been pulled across: a wide, glinting trail that had already frozen over. Sections of this trail sparked red with bits of blood or flesh—flesh that once might have belonged to the squid but, given the state of him, probably belonged to the northerner. More red, ripped flesh rimmed the suckers on the squid's tentacles.

The northerner looked at the shivering crowd. He seemed to be thinking of something to say. His eyes wandered over the inkers, and steam rushed from his nostrils as he pulled his back straight, his chin high. But nothing came to him, or his tongue had frozen solid, so instead of speaking he pulled a knife from his belt and knelt beside his kill. He jammed the blade into the hood, halfway down, and began sawing at the meat. Ice had bloomed in the dead muscle, which made the cutting difficult, and it took many minutes until the northerner had sliced open a section of flesh large enough to reveal the squid's inner workings.

The purple-yellow sheen of tissue and organs was dulled by the cold, but it was visible, and it was horrid. None of the assembled inkers had ever gazed inside a squid's body. They were revolted, and they were angry, but they knew what would happen next, so they did not disturb the northerner as he reached into the beast and began shifting its guts around, poking with his knife, chattering his teeth until he found what he was looking for: the ink sac.

He began sawing more delicately, until he'd released the sac from its membranous connections. With it in hand he stood, lifting it from the corpse and putting the knife aside. It was a small, bulbous organ. There was a dark shimmer through the thin wall of flesh. The northerner raised the sac to eye level and held it out, slicked all over with blood and ice and slime and salt, showing the crowd, grinning and shivering. Ugly victory shone in his ruined features. His teeth parted, his chest swelled, but before he found words one of the gathered inkers barked at him.

Squeeze it!

The northerner's triumph morphed into a frown.

What?

Give it a squeeze, son.

The northerner looked at the organ in his hand, then did as he was told. He pushed his mangled fingers into its contours, and it changed shape, but slowly, strangely, not in the way one would expect liquid to behave. The northerner pulled a glass jar from his pocket, placed it on the ground and held the sac above its opening. He retrieved his knife and, after a hesitation, cut a small slit in it. Nothing fell. Nothing even dripped. He looked up at the crowd of people, who were not moving or speaking. The northerner pushed a finger inside the slit and pulled at it, widening the aperture. Still no ink flowed. Three fingers then dived into the organ, tearing at the membrane, unwrapping it until the contents wobbled gently into the northerner's hand.

It was a lump of waxy, wobbly goo. He let the substance settle onto his palm. It was the same colour as the ink, but of a much duller shade, with no gloss or shine. He poked at it, rubbed it, caressed it, rolled it over and between his fingers, but nothing he did made it act like anything other than soft candle wax. He looked back at the inkers, but they were stumbling back into the pub. He rolled the wax in his hand, turning it into a dark, rubbery sausage, then pulled it into pieces, which he shoved into the many pockets of his over-buttoned jacket. Then the northerner seemed to remember his injuries, his pain, his tiredness. Something bent inside his spine. His shoulders fell and his back slumped. The wind cut at the mouths of his wounds, and he began to shake harder.

Only a few members of the crowd remained. One of them was Zoe's aunt. When the northerner saw her watching him, he flinched. She opened her mouth, not to laugh but to speak, but his words shot out first.

Don't. Please don't.

He stumbled back to his boat, dragging his wounds and the squid into the night.

ZOE LEARNED ABOUT this incident the morning after it happened. She and her aunt walked through the dawn-dark to the pier, where Zoe saw the northerner's trail. She kicked at it, her boot making no mark on the iced gunk. She looked up at her aunt, a question on her face. Her aunt stopped walking. To Zoe, it looked like she was making a decision. Finally, she turned to her niece and explained what had happened the night before.

The ink turns that way when a squid dies, she said. It reverts to the form it takes when the beast is in deep water. Something to do with pressure, and the body going cold.

She sighed, rubbed at her mouth.

He shouldn't have come back.

Zoe took the story in without speaking. She thought of a squid's colours in the moment it released its ink. How death might drain its flesh blank.

Her aunt beckoned her to the pier. Zoe stared at the sheen of bloody slime, and felt herself tighten.

HARD WEEKS PASSED. In the screeching wind and aching-cold sky, winter showed its claws. Elderly members of the town stopped waking up, and people stopped saying the cold snap would pass.

In the eye of the season, a new trouble bloomed. Zoe first became aware of it one evening over dinner. Normally it was just them, but on this night they had guests of a sort—two jars of fresh ink, sitting by their plates.

Her aunt usually sold the ink to one of the wholesalers who waited at the dock each evening. As she chewed, Zoe indicated the ink with her head.

Why's that here?

Tried to rip me off.

Who—Mrs Zhang? Ahmed? Sally?

Yep.

Which one?

All of them.

What?

Her aunt slid her fork into a softened carrot.

They've all gone weird. Offering bugger all.

Why?

Who knows?

Zoe's aunt bit into the carrot, mushing it to paste.

Just a seasonal blip. We'll be right.

She went on eating, sawing at grey beef, flattening limp vegetables. The bottles shook as the table responded to her clattering cutlery, and the ink rocked, forming bright, viscous waves.

Zoe kept chewing. She sipped at some water. She thought

about adding more salt to her food, and tried to forget the questions bobbing in her thoughts.

A blip, her aunt repeated. They'll go back up.

But the price of ink did not float back up—in the following days the prices stayed low, then sank lower. At first the harvesters took it out on the wholesalers, yelling at them, shaking fists, smashing jars of shimmering liquid at their feet. But the wholesalers—all out-of-towners who came in for a day or two to buy ink and take it back to the towns where they lived—could only shrug and apologise, saying that there wasn't demand, that times were tough. This ink is a luxury good, they said, you all know that. People aren't paying for luxuries right now. It's the problems. The state of the country. You know.

If the harvesters did know, they didn't say. They turned from the wholesalers and went home, or drinking, or wherever these problems weren't. Some began selling their hauls at reduced prices.

Zoe's aunt, convinced normal prices would return, kept hoarding hers. The ink bottles multiplied, crowding their dinners. When the ink covered more than half the table Zoe poured too much salt on her beef, and asked one of the questions she'd been trying to forget.

These problems with the ink.

Her aunt grunted.

Is it because of what he said?

Her aunt looked up from her plate.

What? Who?

The northerner.

You spoke to him?

No. He said it when he came here. Something about the rest of the country.

She swallowed: hard gristle, soft throat.

Her aunt sighed.

No, Zo, love. No. That man's not well.

But was he right?

I said no.

Zoe felt a want inside her throat, against the gristly meat, a want to believe her aunt's words. But as the space at their table grew scarcer, she began wondering if the northerner knew something they didn't.

ONE MORNING ZOE'S aunt did not invite her to go inking. She offered no reason—she just got up and left the house, long before Zoe was out of bed. Zoe ate breakfast alone. While chewing her toast she suddenly considered smashing all the bottles of ink on the table, staining the kitchen into a vibrant, grotesque exaggeration of itself. The thought shook, and she pushed it from her mind. Then she pulled on her boots and walked to the white beach on the edge of town.

On her way she noticed that the path to the beach was marred by a slimy, red-iced trail—a trail almost identical to the one her aunt had shown her outside the pub. It followed her, or she followed it, all the way to the shore. Where the asphalt ended it smeared onto the beach. There the trail stopped, but a furrow had been ploughed into the sand, roughly the same width as the shine on the street. Zoe stepped onto the beach. Sand squeaked beneath her rubber soles. She followed the furrow with her eyes, all the way down the shore, until she saw a column of smoke puffing from the wilderness south of the town.

There were no roads or houses in that area. Nobody would be camping there in this weather—nobody sane. But the smoke puffed, a darker grey than clouds. She began to trudge. The smoke solidified in the nearing sky. The temperature dropped, and Zoe needed to keep blinking to stop her eyes icing over. She wondered how the ocean stayed liquid when it was this cold. She hugged her collar to her chin, her hands burrowed into her cuffs. For two hours she followed the furrowed sand towards the darkening smoke, until the beach met a thin stream that ran to the sea through a gap in the hard hills.

She paused, taking in the scrabbled trees, the low slopes

of the foothills, the tannic churn of hill water meeting ocean. Then she lifted her eyes, and saw the smoke climbing in a plume from somewhere upstream.

She turned inland, following the fresh water, and when its path curved she finally found the source of the smoke. A fire had been built on the sand, feeding on long boughs of warped driftwood. Other, smaller fires had been built around the area, and all sat under a range of apparatus: urns, large kettles, and strange clear contraptions of evaporation and titration. Darker smoke rose from these vessels than came from the burning wood. Sacks of coloured powders were scattered among the bubbling concoctions.

It was a scene that would normally command her full attention, but she was distracted by the bodies that lay nearby. A long row of squid corpses had been heaped by the water's edge: huge, slack, porcelain. Zoe had never seen a dead squid before. As she stared at them, and as the rot of their death clawed at her nose and throat, she felt a hollowness expand in her chest. The smoke kept rising from the cauldrons and kettles. The smell grew worse.

One other body was present in the clearing. The northerner sat by the main fire, wrapped in buttons and wool. Much of his face and hands were covered with tabs of plaster or bandages, although some wounds were untreated, scabbing across his cheeks. He was holding a piece of paper, moving his lips as he studied it. He didn't see Zoe until she spoke. Her words came out as a yell.

What are you doing?

The northerner flinched. He looked up, and narrowed his

eyes as they fell on Zoe. Anger came to his face. He crushed the paper and threw it onto the fire.

She sent you, did she? Couldn't be bothered coming herself?

What?

Your mother.

He spat the words, and a cut snapped open on his cheek. He lifted a finger to collect the blood.

Zoe was taken aback by the venom in his voice.

She's not my mother.

The northerner's tone shifted.

Oh.

She's my aunt.

He stood up.

Your mother's dead, then?

Yes.

Heat flashed through Zoe. The northerner wiped at his open wound, regarding her with a look she didn't recognise. Then, in a tone of bitter contemplation, he said: They do that.

Zoe stared at him.

Die. Mothers.

Her cheeks filled with blood. She would have said something, she didn't know what, but the northerner remembered his anger.

Why did she send you? To mock me?

Nobody sent me. Why are you doing this?

Zoe waved an arm at the contraptions, the bodies, hearing the anguish rise in her voice.

You know why I'm doing this. I'm going to modernise...

You've killed them! We never kill them!

Don't you?

He looked at his collection of horrid alchemy.

These things aren't familiar to you?

No! Zoe was crying. The smell was so thick, and the squid were so still.

He gazed over the bubbling pots, the steaming glass.

They're so uncontrollable when they feed, he said. So enraged. He gestured at his face, his hands. You should see what they've done to my boat. You know they have teeth in their suckers? Very hard to remove. Especially when they're thrashing around. You people never seem to get on their wrong side, so I thought it was a technique thing, one I'd eventually figure out. But if you're not even killing them…

He wandered over to one of the urns, where he scooped out a handful of dark wax.

I'm trying to turn this stuff back into ink. But you know how it's done, so if you don't recognise any of this equipment, I suppose I need to start over.

Why?

Zoe kept staring at the urns, the fires, the colourless corpses.

Nobody's paying for ink at the moment. What's the point? Why won't you leave?

The northerner looked up. He took a long breath, but Zoe kept talking, cutting him off.

Was my aunt right? Is someone in your family sick? Do you need money that badly?

When she was done he took another, deeper breath.

No, he said, finally. And yes. Nobody in my family is sick. I don't have a lot of family, to tell you the truth. But I do need money. Very badly. And more importantly, I need to make this work. I need to prove I can do it.

Why?

He smiled at her—a patronising smile, rendered mad by his wounds.

I have investors, he said. Dangerous people, it turns out. They've put a lot of capital into this venture, and if I don't show that it will be successful, they'll be very angry, and I'll be in a lot of trouble.

So it's just money?

Zoe was nearly shouting. She pointed at the corpses.

All this, for a…business idea?

Of course not, he snapped. I'm trying to make it easy for you to understand. It's much more complicated. I've made promises…

A thought crossed his face, and his expression became colder, calculating.

You think I'm cruel, don't you? But I'm no crueller than her.

Who?

Your aunt.

She isn't cruel.

Maybe you're as cruel as she is.

She isn't cruel, Zoe repeated, almost screaming now, her face a messy burn. She just laughs a lot. I don't know why. It's not about you.

No, I'm sure it isn't.

He picked up a stick, and for a moment Zoe thought he was going to hit her. Again she remembered his gun, and panic zipped through her. But he just threw the stick on the fire.

Anyway, he said, I was trying to talk about promises.

He looked at her again.

I'm close. I can sense it. If you were to just tell me—

Zoe cut him off.

When will you leave?

You want this to end?

Of course I do.

He sat back down by the fire. Sand squeaked; embers glowed.

This ends when you let it.

FROZEN, PALLID DAYS, drained of hope, stacked one upon another. Gloom fogged the town. Most of the inkers went on an indefinite hiatus. The rest of the port people lost their routines and fell into states of energetic rage or total listlessness. They stopped parking straight, stopped aiming rubbish at bins. Each morning revealed a worsened place, with worsened inhabitants. The town's doctor was the only one in steady work. Each day his surgery was clogged with alcohol poisoning, frostbite, broken noses and depression. Ice webbed over cracked windows. Loose plastic froze stiff in the gutters.

By midwinter ink prices had been falling for six weeks. That was when the wholesalers stopped coming. They gave no warning—one day they were just not there. Clean, empty slats of wood were revealed in the place on the pier where their stalls usually sat. The inkers who'd been out that day—only four of them, including Zoe's aunt—stood on those strange planks, huffing steam, stomping their feet, waiting not because they believed the wholesalers would appear, but because they didn't know what else to do. Eventually they shuffled off, lugging glass and ink.

The next day Zoe woke to find her aunt ripping a slice of toast apart with slabs of fridge-hard butter, hours after she usually would have left for the sea. They didn't speak. On the table, the swarm of ink bottles shone with a new, peculiar menace.

Zoe did not return to the northerner's camp. At night she dreamed of the squid she'd seen there, death-pale and reeking.

THE TOWN DIED on a Wednesday afternoon, by the doors of the pub. The weeks of despair had seen people drifting there ever earlier, often looking to replace their mid-morning coffee with pints of gravelly stout. The day it closed they were peering through the windows at ten-thirty in the morning, wondering why the lights weren't on, why the stools were still upside down on the bar. They struck the glass with gloved knuckles, but the room stayed dark. One would-be drinker went to the dock and returned with a report: the publican's boat was gone. The publican did not fish, dive, trawl; did not take pleasure in time spent on wide water; had never opened a vein over a wave. His boat hadn't moved in years. The thirsty port people swore, and cried, and pushed their jacketed elbows through a few windows, and stole as much beer as their bellies could hold. Then they went home to pack.

Zoe and her aunt lasted another week. Over dinner on the Sunday, as rain poured down outside, Zoe's aunt laced her fingers together, unlaced them, then moved her fingers up her forearms, rubbing the corrugations of her scars. She drummed the table with a knuckle. She twisted a finger into an ear. When their plates were empty she gathered a breath, looked at Zoe, and began.

Zo, love.

I know.

Relief relaxed her aunt's face.

We'll come back.

When?

I don't know.

Rain hammered the roof, glugged up the windows.

We'll go in the morning.

That night Zoe did not sleep well, even when the rain's pounding lightened into a soft thrum. Too much had happened. She couldn't put what she felt into an order that made sense. Her mind flicked through images, unable to focus on any single one. Her aunt bleeding over the boat. Light bouncing from pink granite, shining on bleached sand. Ink sloshing, bright and dark. The squirm of a puckered gland, the waves of ultra-violet colour on a squid's hood. The pale corpses stretched out where the thin stream met the sea. Wounds fresh and old on the northerner's face. Black smoke wafting; driftwood burning orange and green. Dull buttons hanging from his tattered coat.

They woke the next day to a sky scrubbed clean of clouds. Zoe's aunt blinked up at the blueness.

Let's go for a walk, she said, while we can. Plenty of time to pack.

Zoe's hands were deep in a half-filled backpack, and she felt groggy, but she followed her aunt through the door.

The sun was bright, its heat stronger than it had been in months. The streets were wet with rain and frost melt as they wandered through the town. Occasionally Zoe's aunt would point out a landmark.

That used to be a bakery, she'd say. That's where your mother and I used to throw rocks at the Harris boys. Over there's where the pharmacist fell asleep in the gutter and never woke up. That was your mother's favourite fence. Here's a letterbox she stole, which I made her take back. I once slipped on that corner and shattered my knee.

When they reached the pier Zoe's aunt stepped out onto

the planks. Zoe didn't want to follow her. She was tired, and they would be coming back that way later.

But her aunt yelled: Come on, it won't be the same with our bags, and there was a wistful happiness in her voice, so Zoe did not object. They wandered down towards the boat, marvelling at the lightness of the wind, the pleasantness of the sun, until they heard the splashing.

It was coming from the northerner's boat. Water was being thrown over the side in fast, tenacious bucketloads. They came closer, and saw that the northerner was standing on the deck, shin-deep in ocean, scooping it as fast as he could and tossing it overboard. His efforts didn't seem to be lowering its height.

Unnoticed, they watched him bail on. Occasionally he swore, or spat something they couldn't understand, but mostly he was silent. Zoe felt sadness, and sympathy, and an instinct to leap into the boat and help him. Then she remembered his camp by the stream, and the squid corpses, and what he'd said about her aunt and her mother, and her desire to help vanished as her feet glued themselves to the wood. Her aunt looked on, vaguely fascinated.

Eventually the northerner stopped bailing, straightened up and rested his hands at the small of his back. Water splashed at his knees. He let out a high groan, and as soon as he did Zoe knew what would happen next; she heard the premonition of her aunt's laughter before it escaped her lips. She grabbed at her arm and tried to stop it happening, but it was like herding a wave, corralling a cloud. The laugh pealed out, full-hearted and throaty, and when it reached the northerner he swung around, churning little whirlpools in the boat water.

His face was even more damaged than when Zoe had found him by the stream. He must have given up on plastering the wounds, for they had spread to cover the majority of his exposed skin. Small flashes of white peeked out from the red openings, which Zoe first took to be bone—but as she stared, she saw the curve in their shape, and realised they were the fangs he'd spoken of, the teeth that lived in squid suckers, detached from their tentacles and hanging in his flesh.

Redness burst onto his face as he heard the laughter. The wounds squirmed under his fury. Zoe's aunt kept laughing, and he shouted something unintelligible.

Zoe dragged at her aunt's sleeve, saying: Stop, stop it, stop laughing, but the sight of the northerner heaving his legs through the water only made her aunt laugh harder.

He hauled himself onto the pier, a puddle of limbs and wounds, and her laughter became uproarious, enormous, and Zoe's begs and tugs did nothing, and the sound only stopped when the northerner staggered before them, reached into the rags of his jacket, retrieved his gun and hung it in the air before her aunt's nose.

Zoe's fingers froze in her aunt's sleeve, hooked tight. Her aunt, at last silent, regarded the weapon with surprise and curiosity, but no visible fear. The only movement she made was to loop an arm around her niece, pulling her tight into her side. Zoe's head butted against her aunt's chest. The northerner glared, still short of breath and red of face, and met this movement by raising the gun higher, to her aunt's forehead. A small scream came through his closed lips, and Zoe felt sure that his last rod of northern civility had shattered.

But he only let out another anguished grunt, before lowering the gun. Zoe and her aunt relaxed. Her aunt let her go. She rocked back on her feet as the northerner turned to his boat. Zoe turned to leave. So did her aunt, but not before letting out a final chuckle. It was a small laugh—the faintest pulse of humour—but it was loud enough for the northerner to hear, loud enough to swing him back around. This time, he didn't raise the gun. He just stared at Zoe's aunt; then, in a surge of movement, he shoved her off the pier.

If Zoe had looked at him as her aunt tipped over the edge, she would've seen a grin on his wind-torn lips, a grin carrying satisfaction and revenge and two kinds of victory—over Zoe's aunt and over himself, for limiting his reaction to a shove rather than a shot. But Zoe was watching her aunt fall. She heard her body break the water open. By the time she'd rushed to the edge her aunt's head and hands had surfaced, flinging and twisting, before being dragged back under by the weight of her coat. And by the time the northerner realised he'd done something far worse than he'd intended, Zoe was ripping off her jacket and leaping into the cold ocean to grab at the swirl of fabric drowning her aunt.

She fell, and met ice. The air rushed from her lungs and her flesh blinked numb, and the water that closed over her face stabbed ice into her skull, but she didn't let herself be paused. As soon as her head re-emerged she stroked towards her aunt and grabbed at the mass of thrashing colour. She found the coat, and water, and a floating wave of her aunt's hair, and more water. She pulled at everything her fingers found purchase on, and managed to yank her aunt's head above the surface. Huge gasps shot from her mouth, and her wild arms landed on Zoe's shoulders. Zoe doubled the pace of her kicks, trying to keep them both afloat, but her aunt's body continued to panic, and the roil of their bodies sucked them both under.

In the mess and pain of being underwater Zoe had to extricate herself from her aunt so she could reposition herself behind her, so she could heft her airwards, but her aunt would not let go. Their struggle became manic, and soon it was all Zoe could do to keep her own head above water. She tried to rip the mass of coat from her aunt's shoulders, but her aunt would not stop wrestling the sea. Zoe's lungs burned, and her vision swarmed with lights. Suddenly the weight in her fingers lessened, and the coat floated up before her. She felt relief, and joy, and then nothing but a blank wash of terror as her knee bumped into the bob of her aunt's unmoving body.

The sound of a crash came to her. It seemed far off, but a spray hit her face, bringing the crash somehow closer. More sounds came, hurried splashes; then another body was there, all limbs and speed. Zoe's aunt's face thrust up from the murk. As soon as it appeared it began to retreat from Zoe, pulled away by this new figure in the water, and it was only then, as Zoe was left alone and exhausted in the icy ocean, that she understood the northerner was trying to save her aunt's life.

How well he swam. How easily he parted the waves before him. From all her dealings with him, Zoe would never have imagined him to be this strong in the water. Even with his collection of wounds he was easily chewing up the distance to the shore, Zoe's aunt's body floating pale in his wake. Zoe began to kick after him, slow and sore. By the time her feet bumped into the seabed he already had her aunt laid out on the snowy sand and was kneeling beside her. His hands worked at her sternum, and every few presses he laid a mouth against her aunt's and blew.

Zoe kicked through the shallows towards them. Her aunt was not responding to his attentions, and she could see how tired the northerner was. His speed through the water had come at the cost of his strength, and every breath he wasn't pushing into her aunt's throat was coming out haggard and loud. Zoe slumped down and felt for her aunt's hand. He continued his ministrations for a long time, until he could push and blow no more. He collapsed by her aunt's side, gasping, shivering.

Take over.

He was on his back, not facing Zoe, but she understood. She didn't know how to do CPR, but she moved straight to her aunt, placing her hands near where she'd seen the northerner put his. Fear filled her, but there was no other choice. She stared at her aunt's purpling lips, the stillness of her torso. She pulled in a breath.

Before she could do anything, her aunt moved, or something moved within her. A gurgle came from her throat, and water began to leak from the low corners of her open mouth. Relief began to soar within Zoe, but then she saw that her aunt's eyes remained glassy and frozen, and that she was not coughing. The water rose in her aunt's mouth, a flat pool, blocking any air that she would be trying to draw into her lungs if she were still alive.

Zoe realised she was screaming. Her fingers clawed into tiny buckets, and she began to scoop at the water in her aunt's mouth. She tried to bail out the ocean in her aunt, but for every handful of water she flung away, more swelled to replace it.

Her aunt stayed still. So did the northerner. He had seen what had happened and collapsed back onto the sand beside them. His arms hung loose; his chest heaved. His eyes were open. The sky above them was still blue and clean.

THEY BURIED HER on the beach, at the foot of the dunes where the tide did not reach. The northerner had tried to insist on doing it himself, but Zoe ignored him. Together they gouged a hole into the sand that compacted and darkened and dampened the further down they went. The whole time the northerner was apologising, saying it was an accident. Zoe continued to ignore him, and focused on shifting sand.

It did not take much time to have a grave deep enough to avoid any digging animals and long enough to hold her aunt's body. Zoe took her aunt by the arms. The northerner took her feet. They placed her slowly, awkwardly into the pit, and as soon as the body settled Zoe was scraping and hurling sand onto it as fast as she could. The grave filled quickly. Neither of them spoke.

THAT NIGHT ZOE left the heater on—something her aunt would never have allowed. She did it to stay warm, but also as a reminder. She did not want to fall asleep as usual, unaware of her aunt's wet death. She wanted to stay awake all night, wasting electricity, remembering her aunt. But eventually she drifted off on the couch, her head resting on a pillowless ledge. She woke sweaty and confused, before the memory of it all engulfed her. Then she went looking for the northerner.

First she walked the length of the long beach to his camp, where she found his equipment in disarray. The kettles were upturned and scattered across the banks of the stream. Some of the smaller urns were half-submerged and rusting in the dirt-streaked water. The sacks of powders had been emptied, their contents mixed through the sand. The squid corpses were gone—either removed by hand or devoured by scavenging, winter-starved birds. Zoe took the scene in, made sure the northerner wasn't there, then left.

She went back into the town, and found him alone in the ruins of the pub. He was sitting under the sea-sky painting, burning pieces of broken furniture in the fire, scribbling on a piece of dirty paper. The only light came from the dim sky, which was covered again with clouds, and from the wriggle of the flames.

She crunched over glass, sat on the other side of his table, and stared at the glory of the ink paint until the northerner paused his writing and looked up. She stared into the scabbed wreck of his face. He spoke first.

How are you?

She didn't answer.

Did you sleep?

She crossed her arms. She looked around the room. She looked at the fire, at his letter, at him.

I'll show you.

His pen clattered against the wood. What?

I'll show you how to do it.

Realisation dawned on his face. Why?

Look what happened when we kept it secret.

I didn't meant to…

I know. It was an accident. Do you want me to teach you how it's done?

He screwed up his piece of paper, threw it on the fire.

Of course I do.

THEY TOOK HER aunt's boat. The northerner's wasn't at its dock, and at first Zoe wondered where he'd taken it. Then she remembered, and realised that it must have sunk. If this upset the northerner, he didn't show it. He followed Zoe down the pier, saying nothing.

The sea was calm. They flew across it, taking half as long as a rough-water trip would. They did not speak. When they reached the inking ground she killed the engine. Wake rushed at the bow, and the boat slowed. The northerner looked around, seeing horizon in three directions, the shiny smudge of the dock in the other. Zoe stood up.

Watch what I do, and pay attention, because I'm only going to do it once.

Without ceremony, she revealed the secret of the port to an outsider for the first time. She went through the process slowly, showing him the equipment, the knife, the careful cut into her flesh. She demonstrated the run and drip of her blood. When the squid appeared the northerner flinched, but as it fed and calmed he untensed. Wonder replaced his fear. He helped Zoe net the creature, and squatted by its maw as she blooded its gland and collected the gush of ink. He did not get in her way or badger her with questions. He was silent, awed by what he was seeing. He helped cradle the squid in the water when they released it, his fear of it gone. It was only afterwards, when Zoe turned and spoke to him, that he showed any hesitation.

Your turn.

He baulked.

Now?

We're not going to do this again.

She handed him her knife, handle first.

He took it, looking apprehensive. But he moved to the edge of the boat, and he rolled up his arm, and he unfolded the winking blade of the knife. He looked back at Zoe. She nodded.

Go slow. Just like I showed you.

He looked back to his forearm, hanging over the water. With careful pressure he pushed the metal into the skin, which resisted for the briefest of moments before giving way to the blade. A tear of blood brightened the air, and when it did Zoe put into action the plan she'd been stitching together since the moment her aunt's mouth overflowed with ocean.

With the point of her knife still in the northerner's skin, she gripped the side of the boat with both hands and threw her whole body into a huge push. The northerner jolted, jerked off balance by the sudden rock of the boat, and his errant hand whipped the blade deep into his arm. He yelped, as something cut that shouldn't have, and Zoe felt a swell of pleasure. She hoped the cut was deep. She hoped he thought he would die. This was her revenge—not death, but the fear of it. She wanted him to bleed. She wanted this man to feel so much terror that he changed into something else entirely.

Blood jumped from the wound, high and fast. The northerner grabbed at the rushing flow just as a wave, unseen by either of them, slapped into the rocking boat. Zoe stumbled; one of the northerner's feet tangled in the landing net, and the other slipped in a puddle of blood and water. With no free arms to steady himself he wavered, and wobbled, and crashed over the side.

Zoe rushed to where he'd fallen. His blood was already

clouding the water. She waited for his strong strokes to bring him back to the boat. But the northerner seemed too concerned with his injury to worry about his position in the water. He hung in the salt, eyes wide, face pale, grabbing with increasing feebleness at the opening in his vein.

Here, Zoe called. Swim here!

She cast about for a rope, but by the time she had one in her grip the first squid had caught the scent. It rose from the navy mass and began shovelling the red water into its clacking beak. The northerner kicked away from it, but he only managed to create a clouding trail that summoned a second beast, then a third.

Tentacles cut through the water, herding liquid. More squid rose—more swiping appendages and hungry beaks. The sea's surface was a mess of purple flesh and red-white froth. The northerner finally turned to Zoe, realising what was happening, what could only happen next. He reached for her with the hand of his wounded arm, as his cry for help swirled with brine.

She threw the rope, too short, too wide. The squid found him long before he could swim to it. That was when his screams began: first of terror, then of pain. Suckers fastened onto the meat of him, their cruel external teeth hooked deep, and Zoe learned something that her aunt and the other inkers had never discovered—she learned how they fed when alone.

They took the northerner in a voracious embrace, tentacles draping over his neck and shoulders, while others snaked across him, tasting him, until they found the open source of the blood. Into his arm they weevilled, digging and licking and sucking, tearing him open, carrying rich pieces of him back to their beaks. His screams gave way to gurgles. Golden eyes glowed in the wet. Down he was dragged, under the surface, a mass of tentacles slapping and ripping at him as the growing shoal of squid began to flicker through patterns of glorious bioluminescence.

IN THE YEARS that followed Zoe tried hard to forget the northerner. But he kept appearing to her: his torn face, the bloody thrash of his arm. She tried to push these images away, but they wouldn't leave. Instead, she forgot little pieces of her aunt. She remembered what she had looked like, but not, except for her waterproof harvesting outfit, the sort of clothes she used to wear. She knew the patterns of her aunt's speech, the lilt, the sarcasm, the rhythms, but forgot the words themselves. And her laughter—Zoe knew that the laughter had been there, inexplicable and constant, but what had it really sounded like? Rich and throaty? High and wheezy? A year after leaving the port, Zoe wasn't sure if her aunt had laughed loudly or quietly, and after three years the laugh rang false and harsh in her head, a memory she couldn't trust.

As her aunt dripped away, memory by memory, laugh by laugh, the northerner took up residency in the corners of her thoughts, and would not leave. Perhaps it was because she kept a piece of him with her. When she had returned to the dock, she found something in the boat that she'd forgotten about—the northerner's pistol. Without thinking, she put it in her pocket. It was one of the two things she took when she left the port. The other was a single jar of ink, grabbed from her aunt's table before she followed everyone else heading north.

There she stumbled into the clutches of a military poised to take control of a failing nation. She joined the army, although she wasn't given much choice, and the northerner's pistol made the shift to her hip. That was where it stayed, even when better firearms were made available to her. She didn't try to understand the compulsion. She just kept it, and did not think about why. But while she held it, learned to clean it, care for it, became an expert in its use, she never fired it. Through protests and insurrections it hung idly at her waist, as the various other skills she acquired came to the fore: strategy, intimidation, subterfuge.

Zoe was a phenomenal soldier, a cold revelation in camouflage. She was promoted, again and again, and her life ripped by in a blur of ordered fear, without her ever having to squeeze the pistol's trigger. First she was a private, then a corporal. By the time she was twenty-two she was a sergeant. As she rose through the ranks, as the coup she became part of surged to success, she barely ever pulled the gun from its holster, and never fired it: not until she became a lieutenant, and was sent to a distant mountain in search of a myth.

PART 3

REN'S BODY HIT the ground, and the soldiers surged to their feet. They moved forward, gathering their equipment and the cage as they surrounded their lieutenant and ushered her out of the clearing, through the pines, past the buck-poisoned stream.

At the edge of the forest, Daniel, the young medic, turned back. He saw the villager tearing off his jacket and pressing it against the hole torn in the woman's neck. His son was staring at the retreating soldiers. The boy and Daniel locked eyes for a moment. Then Daniel ran.

He followed his comrades down the mountain in a blinding, green-rinsed rush, down to where the rest of the squad was waiting. They stopped in the village to steal food and fuel, then climbed into their trucks and left town at high speed.

Lieutenant Harker hadn't spoken since she'd fired her gun—actually, Daniel realised, he hadn't heard her speak since they were in the mountain grotto. The silence continued as they sped away: Harker offered no orders to her men.

There was no clear second-in-command, no obvious course of action for them to take. In the end the men jointly decided that they'd drive until nightfall, and make camp somewhere clear and flat where they might be able to contact high command, which they couldn't do in the village. The mountain's loom had been blocking their radio signals ever since they'd arrived.

Around them the pines stayed tall and green, and their scent cut through the blackened smell of the exhaust. Daniel couldn't stop thinking about what had happened on the mountain. Bile raked his throat, and the only thing preventing him from vomiting was the scent of the pines. Straight ahead, he could see one of the other trucks: the one containing the bird's cage. Through the windows, he could see that the black cloth was still in place.

The trucks clattered through the day. When the sun hit the trees they pulled over beside a wide, slow river and pitched their tents on its bank. Someone lit a fire. Another made a great show of scouting a perimeter. Lieutenant Harker sat by the placid water. Daniel watched her. He felt calmer now, and tired, and he remembered that despite everything, he was still her medic.

He walked over and crouched beside her, noting the red gape of her eyeless socket, thinking that it was a sight he might never get used to. He saw the rusty patina of blood on her face, and wondered for a moment if tears would be warm or salty enough to cut through its crust, before realising the cruelty of such a thought.

Daniel turned to face the river. He could hear her breaths coming short and fast. He waited until they slowed before speaking.

You know I need to dress it.

She dipped her neck in a tight nod.

It would be better to do it tonight. Infections. Blood loss. You know.

Again she nodded.

Now he had her permission, Daniel did not test her with any more words. He fetched his kit and helped her lie on her side. The sound of the river lapped at his ears as he cleaned the wound, swabbing at the contours of the socket, disinfecting the area, noting the neatness of the severed viscera, before stuffing soft gauze into the aperture and gliding her eyelid closed over it. Through these ministrations she did not protest, did not scream, although the whole time she was shaking, wincing, sometimes jerking away from his touch. Sweat salted her face and slimed at his grip, but he kept working, wiping his hand on the soft grass of the riverbank. When he was finished, he helped her sit up.

She lifted a thumb to the gauze.

Thank you.

Of course. But you must be in a lot of pain.

He held out two tubes of pills.

You need to take these. These are for pain, he said, shaking the first tube. And these are for infections, shaking the other. Take two each, every morning, afternoon and night. And drink lots of water, eat some food.

He put the pills at her feet, and passed her a bottle and a pack of rations.

She angled her chin away from him.

Okay, said Daniel. Okay.

It was clear that he should leave, so he stood up and washed his hands in the river, rinsing them hard and cold up to his elbows. He wondered if in the next day, and the ones that followed, he'd feel different: if putting distance between themselves and the mountain would change anything inside him. Then he went to his tent and crashed to sleep, his boots still on.

IN THE DEEP early morning his torso snapped up, a harsh awakening. Once he'd oriented himself he tried to go back to sleep, but found that he couldn't stop recounting everything they'd done on the mountain. How they'd weakened the deer trap by sawing at its tripwire. How they'd stomped coarse camping salt into the loam of the hermit woman's garden; how a zucchini had exploded under the heel of his boot. He thought of the ease at which rings of bark had come away from the trees, and how, in a green meadow splashed with purple and white flowers, they'd blasted apart a grazing buck and dumped the mangled corpse in the stream by the cave. How these plans of pressure and torture had come so smoothly from their lieutenant, as if she'd decided on them long before she ever came to the mountain or met the woman living there.

He thought of how this approach—this methodical disintegration of resistance—was consistent with the way they'd behaved during the coup. Their squad was known for subtle tactics, led by their lieutenant's uncanny nous for strategy, her nose for manipulation. She had moulded them into ambushers, infiltrators, outflankers. By the end of the coup they were primarily being used for shadow missions, spilling little blood but achieving significant victories. Minimal fuss or collateral damage. It was why Zoe Harker was celebrated—or mistrusted, if you asked the more bloodthirsty members of the military hierarchy—and almost certainly why her squad had been chosen for this mission.

Daniel could not fault their actions, nor did he think he would have acted differently had he been in charge. He had, he remembered, not hesitated to swing the butt of his rifle into the hermit's jaw the moment she began to disturb their plan on the mountaintop. Yet Lieutenant Harker obviously hadn't planned to have one of her own eyes torn out. Nor did he believe that she had planned to shoot the woman they'd tortured.

A gnaw started in his stomach. He felt afraid, although he wasn't sure of what. Initially he thought this fear was for himself, now that their lieutenant's wounding had compromised their mission. But then he came to realise that his fear was for her, and from the fact that there was little he could do to help her. He owed her so much. She was cold, yes, but she was also smart and merciful and, with one recent notable exception, nonviolent. He knew he was lucky. He could've been sent anywhere when the army yanked him out of medical school and threw him into a uniform, but it was in her squad that he ended up.

He'd hated being forcefully conscripted: hated the idea of hurting people, of the hardship and monotony of soldiering. He had slow reflexes, and got no thrill from the adrenaline rush of danger. He'd assumed that he'd die early, had tried to prepare himself mentally for it. And without Harker's planning and presence, he would have, many times over.

Again he remembered her on the mountain—standing tall, until a mythical bird tore her down. Others thought her aloof, but he knew that she cared for them: that they all still lived was proof of this. Now that she was maimed, it was his job to care for her, and he didn't know if he could.

He thought of how cool and quiet she'd been as he swabbed at her wound, even as she winced in pain. Sleep took hours to reclaim him.

HE ROSE WHEN the sun did. Out in the lowland air he found Lieutenant Harker sitting not by the river, but by the fire. She was hunched towards it, her arms crossed over her knees. In one hand she held the pill bottles he'd given her the night before. They were full, and their caps looked unopened. He sat down, and was about to remind her to take them, how often and how many, when she spoke in a low and ragged voice.

Do you think she survived?

Who?

The woman. On the mountain.

Oh. I don't know.

You're a medic.

A memory flashed in his mind: his rifle butt cannoning into the woman's chin, her head falling to slap at the mountain's stone. Another scene quickly replaced it: Harker shooting the woman as she knelt in the clearing.

It's hard to say. I didn't get a good look at the wound.

The lieutenant turned her eye on him, fixing him in place until he swallowed and spoke again.

You shot her in the throat. She's dead, lieutenant.

Harker stood and lurched off, her steps heavy and grace-less. Daniel felt a sudden need to call after her, but found that he couldn't say anything, not even to ask her about the pills. He sat there, watching the fire until the embers blinked black and the other soldiers woke up.

DURING THE NIGHT one of the soldiers had managed to speak with high command. Details of the mission had been passed on—the capture of the heron, the lack of radio signal, the incapacitation of the lieutenant—and, after a short time, their commanding officers had come back with orders. Eight of the squad had been ordered to the nearest city, where they would join a larger force that had been sent to quell unrest in the region. A group of guerrilla fighters had been shooting truck drivers and throwing pipe bombs into post offices.

The other four soldiers were exempt. High command recognised the value of the bird, and wanted it taken straight to its intended destination: a formerly abandoned animal sanctuary, newly restored under the military regime, in the far eastern reaches of the country. Due to her injury, Lieutenant Harker would stay away from combat and remain with the heron as its escort. With her would go Daniel, in case her condition worsened, and one of the squad's scouts, to help guide the way. The final member of the group was a tall, wide-chested private, chosen by high command without comment. Daniel remembered that this private had been the one to kill the buck and spread its entrails across the mountain woman's stream. He had done so with more gusto than was necessary—had enjoyed the work, had done it well.

As soon as these orders had been passed on, the soldiers broke camp. They packed their tents, kicked out the fire, checked and loaded their weapons. All but the selected four lost their confusion of the previous day and fell into habits formed by their training. Sluggish steps became swift strides; indecision became assurance. In fifteen minutes they were finished. Their trucks spat to life. They glanced at their lieutenant and the men who were to stay with her. A few looked like they might say something, but in the end none did. They let their tyres bite dirt and drove off, leaving the remaining quartet with a single truck, a stack of supplies, some containers of fuel, and a black-wrapped, leaking cage.

Dust rose from the road and came to settle in a film on the river's face. Lieutenant Harker had her eye closed and was pushing deep breaths through flared nostrils. The scout, a bony youth who rarely spoke, had opened his pack and was rummaging through it. The tall private kept his eyes on the receding trucks, watching until they diminished into nothing.

Daniel looked towards the river, at the thick reeds in its shallows, at the dust on the surface. He was waiting for orders until he remembered that, technically, he was a sergeant. The rank hadn't been gained through action or deeds—they'd given it to him only because of his medical skills. It dawned on him that, due to Harker's incapacitation and his rank, he had become the de facto leader of their group.

A strange feeling came over him—as if he was witnessing this point in his life from a distance. He was a farm boy, a rural bookworm who'd dreamed of becoming a doctor, maybe a surgeon. The only authority he'd ever imagined wielding had been over nurses handing him scalpels. Yet he was about to order killers down a highway.

He wanted to laugh, or scream: he wasn't sure which. But he turned to the other three and tried to think of something sensible to say.

Thoughts knotted his mind, and a weight sagged his

tongue. He had never been good at coming up with ideas or speaking in public. Just as words were beginning to straighten in his throat the scout emerged from his pack, holding a many-folded sheet of paper.

Got it, he said. Look.

He unfolded the paper, revealing a splash of colours intersected by a grid of black lines.

We're here.

He pointed at a blue line snaking through a splodge of deep green.

And we need to get there.

His finger slid to the other side of the map, over more green and blue and yellow and into a patch of dense whiteness.

That's where the sanctuary is.

Daniel nodded.

Okay. We had better get going.

His voice sounded small in his ears. He turned to Harker.

Lieutenant?

She moved her chin up and down without opening her eye.

Okay, he repeated. Okay.

It occurred to him that he was always saying okay. He looked at the map, at the truck, at the river, back at the map.

You drive, he said to the private, who nodded, but did not move.

None of them did until the scout, finally realising that his role in all of this was expanding, raised an arm towards the road.

It's this way.

They packed their gear into the truck. It was Daniel who hefted the heron's cage, holding it at arm's length, waiting for something to happen. Nothing did. The bird might have been sleeping, if sleeping was something it did. As he swung it into the truck, he noticed how the private flinched as the cage came near him. Daniel looked at him, surprised—the private was the sort of man who prided himself on not flinching. He hadn't blinked as he eviscerated the peaceful buck in the mountain meadow. But now his eyes were wide, his skin pale, his whole body tense. He was staring at the cage, his mouth slightly open. From under the cloth there came a faint gurgle, the sound of a stream breaking on a stone. The private flinched again. Daniel would have laughed—he did not like the private much—if he hadn't also flinched at the sound and the way the cage shook in his grip. He carefully placed it in the back seat of the truck and got in beside it.

Not long after they began driving the bird became active, perhaps woken by the bumps and vibrations caused by the corrugations in the road. The first sign of its displeasure was the temperature in the truck, which at first crept, then plunged downwards. They began to shiver, even Lieutenant Harker, and fog began misting from their mouths. Ice clawed at windows, mirrors, the faces of their watches. They turned up the heat, blasting stale warmth from the vents, but the bird responded by abandoning its ice wave and instead puffing clouds of steam from beneath the cage's curtain. Their shivering ceased, replaced by noisy panting. Their skin swapped goosebumps for streams of sweat.

Daniel passed Harker a bottle of water, which she did not drink. The scout wiped his face with a small towel he'd fished from his pack. The private refused to take his eyes off the road, even as his hands shook and his breathing shallowed. They turned off the heat and cranked down the windows. A breeze whipped into the truck, bringing the temperature back to normal, and within moments the bird reverted from leaking steam to breathing frost.

This cycle of heat and ice continued into the afternoon, through four hours of driving, and all of it happened with the black oilcloth still fastened over the cage. Daniel knew he should say or do something, but he had no idea what. The day wore on, hot and cold and bitter. The constant alternation between shivering and sweating distracted him, and the only way he could remain calm was by staring out at the country around him.

For the first few hours they had snaked through the foothills of the mountain ranges. The river they'd camped by was in sight at most times. Whoever built the road had designed it so its contours matched the course of the water. After a while the forest thinned, and the trees gave way to pastures of long grass. Weak fences, sagged with loose wire, cut these fields into what could have been farms, but there was no livestock, no crops, no machinery, no farmers. The grass had claimed the land, pushing stalks high and wide, obscuring all signs of worked soil. Soon after entering these wild fields the road doglegged, and over this bend Daniel saw the river's death.

Below a thistled hill it met a sudden scatter of rocks, and on their smooth faces it crashed, foamed and split into five tributaries. Two were substantial, almost new rivers in themselves, but the other three weren't much more than brooks, almost trickles. All ran in different directions. The road followed one of the smallest, a stream which became a creek, which seeped into one of the lowest, greenest paddocks and must have then dived underground, through gaps in limestone or shale, for it did not come back into view.

Daniel told the private to pull over for lunch. As the truck stopped beside the road he took a long, moist-hot breath— the bird was in a steam phase—and lurched out of his seat. In the welcome freshness of the grassy air he walked to the nearest fence and rested his hands on a strand of stiff bent wire. The unkempt fields stretched to the horizon in every direction except for the way they'd come from, where the forests and mountains were now distant outlines against the sky. The wind was soft and slow. Clouds were thick above him, grey cotton shading greyer.

It reminded him of his home, of the little farm he'd grown up on, near the other side of the country. That farm had always been brimming with activity. He remembered wondering as a child if his parents ever slept. More idle memories rolled through him, days of harvest and shearing, dogs barking, dinners roasting in a hot kitchen. Sometimes, during the coup, he had caught himself looking forward to returning to the farm, helping his father fix the fences, doing all the chores he'd hated as a child.

He gazed out at the abandoned fields, fiddling with these memories, until he remembered the mountain, and despite the pleasant sensation of the wind on his skin he felt wildly angry, and he wanted to twist the fence wire in his hands, to rip it apart.

Soon he became aware that Lieutenant Harker was standing beside him. He hadn't heard her approach—she was just there.

In slowness, her grace remained. Daniel straightened up and offered her some of his water, which she did not take. He tried to force a light tone into his voice.

That bird's something else.

What was her name?

Sorry?

Her name. The woman on the mountain. The one I shot.

I don't know. I'm sorry.

Someone must have known.

It's possible.

Lieutenant Harker shook her head.

I never asked. It didn't seem important.

Daniel didn't know what to say. He wasn't sure if he should say anything at all. Minutes passed, until he broke the silence.

Have you taken those pills? You really need to, every couple of hours, like I said yesterday when—

Harker cut him off.

Do you think we're being followed?

She had turned back to face the direction they'd come from.

What?

He looked at the road and saw no sign of vehicles. Nothing but gravel and the land all around it.

By who?

He waited for her answer, but she had apparently become bored of the topic. She walked back to the truck. The scout and the private joined her. The private turned the engine on. Daniel stared back at the road, still seeing nothing. He drifted back to the truck and got in. The private pulled back onto the road.

Daniel waited for the bird to engulf them with mist or steam, but none came. In the front, the scout kept studying his map.

With no river to follow the road blanded out into a long, turnless ribbon. The lack of water changed the landscape; as the hours stacked up, the pastures lost their greenness, fading into beige and hazel. They flattened, losing the humps and rocks of the foothills, and their fences straightened and strengthened, gridding the land into stiff fields. There was still no sign of people. The fields poured on, yellow and dry, and their blondness began to feel eternal. No mountains rose in the distance now, no hills, just a weak tide of golden crests undulating towards the fuzz of the horizon.

Nobody spoke. The bird stayed dormant, and Daniel was able to relax into the drive. He avoided looking in the mirror, at the cage or private or lieutenant, and concentrated solely on the world through the windscreen. The road was a black-grey thread cutting through the yellow fields. Tiredness scratched his eyes. The truck and the hours rolled on.

The scout fell asleep, his many-folded map open on his chest. At some point the sun lowered to the height of the window, its streaks of light lengthening as it died into the horizon. This light hit Daniel's eyes, shook him alert, told him they needed to find somewhere to camp. He began scanning the fields for signs of a stream, little dips or valleys or concentrated greenery.

Soon he saw something better. It came out of the horizon as a wavering dark block, a slate smudge rising from the blond fields. When they came closer he could see what it was, and that it was built with huge, roughly cut grey stones. Thick mortar pasted them together beneath a shingled roof. Dirty windows, gleaming at regular intervals along the walls, revealed nothing about the interior.

He raised a hand towards the house.

Pull in there.

The private steered the truck onto the gravel driveway that led towards it, and the shifting of their course, or the new angle of the strafing sun, awoke the scout. He blinked, stretched, rubbed his face. Lieutenant Harker remained silent.

The private parked at the back, keeping the building between the truck and the road. The apparatus of a well revealed itself in a nearby field. Daniel, feeling confident at the discovery of the house, told the scout to check if the well was dry, then turned to the lieutenant.

I thought we'd stay here tonight.

Harker looked exhausted, as if she'd spent the day marching in high heat. Daniel was thinking of something else to say, something that would put her at ease, but nothing came to him. Then he heard the driver's door shut.

The private was moving towards the house in a fast, scurrying crouch, holding his rifle high. Daniel began to shout something, a question, but the private turned to him with a furious look. He raised a finger to his lips and held up a flat palm. He resumed his approach, moving fast and quiet. He eased the door open, peered in, rifle held to his eye, then disappeared inside.

Daniel felt anger grip him. He turned to the lieutenant, who was leaning back in her seat, her eye closed. He was trying to figure out what to do, if he should do anything at all, when she spoke.

He's clearing the building. Anyone could be in there. Guerrillas, dissidents, deserters. Scared farmers with shotguns.

She said it calmly, her voice unworried. Daniel felt his pulse quicken. It was suddenly so obvious.

It doesn't matter, Harker said. If anyone's in there, they've already seen us.

Panic rushed at Daniel. His eyes flashed to the windows of the house, which were dark and revealed nothing. He felt the need to act, but he didn't know what to do. More than anything, he wanted Lieutenant Harker to rise from her seat and fix things. The old Harker would never have approached this house, never have got them into a mess like this. But now she just sat there, eye closed, breaths even.

The old Harker, Daniel thought, would never have shot the woman on the mountain.

The sound of a clap snapped through the air. Daniel looked up to see the private, who was standing in the doorway to the house, wearing a wide grin. Daniel felt relief course through him and got out of the truck. Behind him the scout was returning from the well with two heavy buckets, also smiling, and all of it made Daniel feel strangely happy. Harker levered herself out of the truck, and the relief inside Daniel renewed his confidence.

He faced the private.

Good work. And lieutenant, he said, I really must insist you take those pills. Not the painkillers, if you really don't want to, but definitely the antibiotics. We can't have you getting infected.

She looked at him with the same detached calmness that hadn't left her face since they'd come down from the mountain. He tried to hold a posture that matched the authority in his words. He was so preoccupied with this that he didn't see her swinging fist.

He probably would have missed it even if he'd been paying attention. It came so fast, flying in a hard blur, that he didn't even have time to flinch. But her knuckles went wide, not even scraping his chin. She had misjudged the distance.

He stepped back, a yelp jumping from his throat. Harker was swaying on her feet, staring at her hand. They both stood still. The scout and the private hung back. Harker looked up at Daniel, whose face had flushed red.

I'm sorry, he said. I…

This time her fist came in a straight jab: a strike that did not contend with depth. A crack rang loud, bone on bone, as her knuckles whipped into his jaw. He stumbled backwards, rocked into a crouch. Blood ran from his lip. Harker turned and walked into the house.

Nobody mentioned the punch as they unpacked the truck. There was enough space for all of them to sleep in the main downstairs area, but the lieutenant dragged her kit up the stairs to an empty smaller room. The scout drew three more buckets of water from the well as the private lit a fire in the cold hearth.

When the first logs had burned through, Daniel, who hadn't spoken since the lieutenant struck him, unpacked some collapsible bowls, filled them with well water and set them by the coals. Once they were boiling he added a few sachets of dehydrated food—peas and legumes and nutrient powders. As they waited, the three of them unrolled their sleeping kits, washed their faces, sipped water. The food was still not ready, so they sat on the hard, dusty floor, not talking until Daniel at last said: I guess I'd better bring it inside.

The scout shrugged. The private stared at the boiling bowls. Daniel stood up, returned to the truck, reached inside and only looked at the cage long enough to make sure he was grabbing a steady handle. His lip stung, and he could taste the copper of his blood. He pulled the cage swiftly out of the back seat and marched back to the house, holding it at arm's length, waiting for steam or ice to shoot out. But the bird played none of its tricks, and he made it back into the house without incident. He sat the cage against a far wall.

The private stood and made a show of stretching, then casually—too casually—positioned himself as far away from the cage as he could. The scout watched the cage carefully, the smallest expression of wonder on his face. Daniel finished his soup and fell asleep.

SOMETIME IN THE night a storm cracked the sky apart. Daniel was woken by thunder. The rain drummed into his mind, taking him from sleep into a state of confused semi-wakefulness.

In this half-dream he saw his family farm, and what it was like when too much rain fell on the fields. The ground would soften and squelch, and when it was completely soaked the worms and bugs that lived in the dirt would squirm to the gasping surface. Their appearance would summon hungry frogs. Small eels would join them, gliding from heavy streams over the wet soil and grass. The glisten of the frogs and eels would bring long-legged waterbirds to feast on them—murderous egrets, picking their way through the muddy banquet. Their bills darted, their bellies ballooned, and for some of them flight became an obvious discomfort.

As the slick frogs and eels feasted on the invertebrates, and as the birds feasted on them, the rodents and small marsupials would flee to higher, drier parts of the farm—the humps and hills that rose from the wet-dark fields like mossy islands. There they scurried for shelter under gorse and eucalypts, and if they could find none they waited for one of two things: for the water to recede, or for death, because while there was plenty of rich grass to eat, there were also plenty of raptor shadows tracing their movements across the ground. Kites, falcons, goshawks and harriers were drawn from far skies. They took turns to dive, to sink their talons into warm flesh, to rise to branches where they lunched on their damp kills.

Under heavy rain, the farm thickened with life and death. Daniel was so young back then, a small figure clad in plasticky overalls and waddling in orange gumboots. He splashed through the mud and water, unaware of what it meant for grain, rot, the integrity of topsoil and riverbanks. In his half-sleep he saw his father's face, smiling at his careless splashes. His father's mouth opened, but the words did not reach Daniel's dreaming ears. Something was too loud. Everything was too loud. Thunder exploded, and suddenly he was fully awake, fully grown, hot and scared in his sleeping bag, fumbling for his bearings.

Out of nowhere, said a voice.

Daniel turned to its source. Lieutenant Harker was sitting close to the fire. Two fresh logs were crackling on a bed of embers. She was holding her knees to her chest, looking into the flames.

The storm, she said. It came out of nowhere.

Daniel nodded. He looked over at the scout and the private. They were asleep. Then he looked at the windows, at the rain spattering against the glass. He rubbed his face, slowly waking up.

I'm sorry, said Harker.

She pointed at Daniel's face. He realised he was rubbing the part of his jaw she'd struck earlier in the day.

It's fine.

No, it's not. I shouldn't have done it.

I understand, he said.

I doubt you do. But thank you. It won't happen again.

Daniel had never heard her apologise. All the time he'd been with her, she'd never had cause to. He didn't know what to say, and although he'd been hurt by her blow, he felt a heat in his guts as she spoke to him this openly. He felt he had to say something meaningful in response.

What you've done for me—for the other men as well—you could hit us all, a couple of times a day for a few months at least, and we'd…

This rain, she said. Remarkable. Did you see how dry the land was, on the drive today? Can't have rained for weeks.

Daniel could only nod.

If there were any farmers around, Harker continued, they'd be thrilled.

She underarmed a stick onto the fire.

Or not, I suppose. You know how farmers are with rain. Never enough, or far too much.

I grew up on a farm.

Is that right? Anyone still there?

My parents are there. And a few hands.

Are you sure?

Daniel felt his skin flush, and indecision crept into his foggy mind.

Shit, Harker said. I'm sorry. Again. I didn't mean it like that. I'm sure your farm is fine. I just meant…You saw how empty those fields were today. If you grew up on a farm, you'd know that this is supposed to be the rainy season.

She pointed at the window.

It should be like this all the time.

Daniel looked at the falling storm.

I suppose so.

But it was all so dry, wasn't it?

Yes.

Makes you think.

Does it?

I don't know.

She leaned back, stretching her arms behind her head. Her fingers arched with slow symmetry, and it reminded Daniel of the poise that used to fill all her movements. She held the stretch for a minute. More lightning flashed at the window. Another crack of thunder came through the walls, and the rain became heavier. Harker let her hands fall back to the floor. She turned her head to look at the cage.

Must be the bird.

Daniel followed her gaze. Beneath the black cloth the shape was barely discernible, and it didn't seem to be moving. But then another fork of lightning flashed, and when it did the cage gave a small shake. Not the lurch of something disturbed, but a settling, something like contentment. The edges of the cloth flared upwards. The cage rocked, then settled as its curtain corrected itself. When the corresponding thunder followed the cloth fluttered again, this time pushed by a waft of happy vapour.

Daniel thought about what he knew of rain herons—how in the stories they were associated with rainfall, abundance and harvests, but also with floods and destruction, sometimes death. The rain drummed on and the cage trembled.

He looked back at Harker.

Why do they want it?

Who?

The generals. Or whoever's in charge.

She shrugged.

Men want things. They hear about something and pretty soon they're convinced it belongs to them.

A few minutes passed, filled with storm noise and the odd burst of sparks as the heat of the fire found veins of sap in the logs. Harker poked at the coals with the toe of her boot.

It's not going to change anything.

After that she stopped talking, and gave no sign that she would say anything more. Daniel wanted her to continue, but he didn't know how to ask, or what to say. He stared again at the cage, until he thought of a question she could answer straight.

How did you know?

Harker looked up, her face glowing orange.

Know what?

That it'd be up there.

She hunched forward.

I didn't. Not when we were given the mission. Not when we arrived on the mountain.

But you must have. What you did to that woman—

What we did.

Yes, what we did—

I didn't know until I talked to her.

How?

Harker rubbed her chin, and did not speak for a long moment. Then she said: I followed the boy up the slopes, thinking that I'd find a crazy hermit who was out of her mind, who knew nothing, and we'd all be able to leave. But I was wrong. She wasn't crazy. She was furious, and determined, and so worried that I'd hurt the boy. And she was smart. There was no reason for her to be living up there like that. So I thought: there must be something. A reason why she was there. And when I asked her about the bird, she laughed at me, and her laugh was forced. So I knew. I hadn't been expecting to find anything, but I did. I suppose I could have pretended I didn't.

Why didn't you? And why did you—

She cut him off, snapping a hand above the flames.

I thought I was doing her a favour. It sounds crazy, I know. But if I had pretended I didn't know she knew about the bird, if we returned to headquarters and reported that, they would have sent someone else. Maybe not immediately, but eventually someone would have gone to the mountain in our place, and whoever they sent would have torn the information out of that woman we found in ways...You know their ways. They would have burned the soles of her feet. Carved her ears off. Killed that man and his boy, slowly, in front of her. I told myself that if I did it my way it would make her life miserable, but she would live. They would all live. I thought it best. And then...

She gestured at the gauze on her face, at the gun on her hip.

Maybe you're right. We should have left straight away.

Daniel leaned back on his pillow, and tried to match the rhythm of his thoughts to the pounding of the rain. He closed his eyes to the cracks of lightning. When the thunder snarled, he tried to let it chase him into sleep. But it took a long time.

He kept thinking of what Harker had told him, about the hermit they'd harried, about their time on the mountain. The sweet menthol of the air, the horror they'd brought to that woman. And in his drowsy mind it began to mix with what he'd been dreaming about before he woke: his family farm, bloated with rain. He saw himself on the mountain, hollow in the cheeks, rigid with ropey muscle, a gun in his hand; and then he saw himself before it all, as a child gambolling through muddy puddles; then as a slow-striding youth, dreaming of growing up to wear a coat and a kind expression as men and women came to him, anxious and worried, before being healed by his soft smile and flawless counsel.

The storm crashed on. Every now and then his eyelids flicked open, reacting to its sound and light. The last time they did, he saw Lieutenant Harker leaning over the fire. It occurred to him that this was how he kept seeing her—sitting down, staring at coals. Once again she was holding the tubes of pills he'd given her. Relief lapped at his drowsy mind, as did a small throb of victory, until he saw what she was doing.

The tubes were open, and she was upending them towards her free palm. The pills fell one by one, and as each landed in her hand she flicked it with a hard thumb into the fire. They landed on glowing coals, where they fizzed, blackened and crumbled into soot.

Daniel could smell them burning—an acrid taint to the damp static of the air. The scent followed him into sleep.

MORNING CAME, BRIGHT and rainless. The water that had pelted down during the night lay in wide puddles across the road and fields, but the sun was already working on drying them. As the soldiers laced their boots outside the house they were hit by moist warmth, rising from the gravel.

They moved to the truck, throwing in their gear. Daniel placed the cage on the ground by the back of the vehicle as he and the other men stowed their equipment. They were about to leave when they noticed Harker hanging in the driveway, staring at the direction they'd travelled from the previous day. The three of them paused. Daniel turned to the scout.

Do you think we were followed yesterday?

The scout frowned.

By who?

I don't know. Just a thought. Did you notice anything?

The scout shook his head.

No, although I wasn't looking.

He too looked at the road, and at the puddles in the gravel.

It'll be hard to see if someone is following us today. The water will stop dust rising from the road. But I'll keep an eye out.

Daniel nodded. He was about to thank the scout when he heard a loud shout. He jumped in shock, and turned as another shout reached his ears, then another.

They were coming from the private. His face wore a terrified expression, and he was staring at his left boot, which was half-submerged in a puddle. A layer of ice covered the surface of the water and clung to the boot, anchoring the private's leg to the ground.

Daniel stared at the frozen puddle, noting that the ice was unbroken, that it must have formed in the seconds after the private had trod in the water. The private yanked at his leg, still yelling, as Daniel saw the trail of frost glinting across the driveway gravel, running in a wide smear to the heron's cage.

Before Daniel, the scout or Harker could do anything the private shouted again, a noise heavier with fear than his others had been, and fired his rifle at the cage. The shots exploded in Daniel's ears. A flurry of bullets rattled through the bars, ripping holes into the black cloth.

Stop!

Daniel blinked. The word had not come from him or Harker, but from the scout. The private stopped firing, and the scout sprinted towards the cage, hurling his long military coat over it, just as a thick finger of mist began snaking through one of the newly torn apertures. He threw his arms around the cage's frame, pulling his coat tight, using the woollen belt to tie it firmly in place. He did all this with a peculiar degree of tenderness.

When it was done the scout stood up, breathing heavily. Adrenaline had washed pinkness into his cheeks. He and the private—rifle now lowered, foot still iced stuck—were staring at each other. Everyone stayed quiet, until the silence was broken by Harker's laughter.

She was bent over, her chuckles thick, throaty. Daniel watched her, and then he was laughing, too. So was the scout. A smile covered his flushed face, and although his laughter was quiet and withdrawn, it still spilled out into the damp morning air. Only the private did not laugh—not until he kicked his boot free of the ice. The effort made him stumble, and finally he joined his comrades in laughing at the madness of it all, his voice strangely high for such a large man.

Daniel felt slightly manic, but also light, somehow loose. He watched his lieutenant, how she smiled, how she wiped at her forehead. How her face had taken on a mild glow.

THEY LEFT THE property soon after, and found that the world they'd gone to sleep in had been changed by the night's wet violence. Muddy puddles reflected the bright-clouded sky, giving the land an illusion of greater depth and texture. Greenery showed itself in fresh shoots that had lain dormant in the dry earth. Vapour wafted up from the soggy paddocks, slanting their view of the land in the distance. In the changed nature of it all Daniel was reminded of the storm of the previous night, and what Lieutenant Harker had said to him about his parents' farm.

He pictured his mother feeding the dogs, his father driving out to the milk shed, stopping every so often to hoe at this-tles poised to seed. He tried to think of what they'd be saying when they ran into each other throughout the day, but the little phrases they used together—the verbal tics that each family develops, ones he used to know so well—wouldn't come to him. If he heard them spoken out loud, they'd be familiar. Even just one, a simple comment from his mother to his father, and he'd know them all, every little piece of the uniquely textured lexicon that threaded their lives together. He imagined their busy bodies, their moving mouths, but the images came to him in silence.

Daniel decided that he'd go see them as soon as the mission was over. He'd go straight to the farm. Light bounced from a puddle and shone into his eyes, rousing him from his thoughts. He tried to return to them, to remember how his parents spoke, but as the truck took the next bend he was distracted.

The truck swerved around a sharp corner and was greeted by a steep descent into a tunnel of dense, dark foliage. The road plunged and twisted, and above them the light was obscured by leaves. Daniel stared out the window, trying to come to terms with this abrupt change of landscape. The vegetation was hedge-like, with sharp, glossy leaves and a paucity of visible branches. Red berries blinked in the green. A wild-holly hedge, thought Daniel.

After the third or fourth bend the leaves thinned, and he could see larger plant life beyond them. At the sight of a large spreading canopy the word *oak* occurred to him, and when a group of skinny, white-black mottled trunks shot up straight he thought *birch*. More trees blinked through the holly hedge, shapes of wood he could not name. Occasionally he saw a steely flash of rock, or cloud, or a body of water.

They continued to lose height, dropping into a valley. When the road flattened and straightened the holly gave up its grip on the asphalt and pushed back from the truck, allowing the true forest to show itself.

The dark hug of the hedge had given their descent a touch of gloom, a feeling almost subterranean. But now there was light, and air, and Daniel could see the spreading oaks and elms that lay beyond the holly, and the copses of birches and gnarling walnuts and other trees. A forest breathed around them, dappled and wide. Beyond its border lay steep hills, much like the one they had driven down. The forest attempted to climb up these valley walls, but made it less than halfway. Where the trees ended lay mossy meadows, cut apart by ancient fences of rough-stacked stone. These meadows rose at harsh angles into rounded fells, ending in domed peaks of hazy grass. They were clouded here and there by sheep, or perhaps goats, although no shepherds could be seen.

They drove on. Nobody spoke, although Daniel was sure that the others felt what he did—the disquieting sense of having emerged from a cave or woken up in a strange house. The glossy green of the hedge, the varied greens of the trees and the pale green of the meadows combined to overwhelm his vision with verdant colour. It was only the white specks of sheep on the fells and the occasional blueness of the sky that kept him from feeling dizzy. Still, he felt wrong-footed, confused at the lushness of the place, until the truck rounded yet another corner, and a large lake cut into view.

It stretched for at least a few kilometres, running from the holly hedge to the base of a far-off fell. Its surface was a sharp grey, untroubled by wind or wave. Small islands, thick with trees, hung anchored towards its centre. The road ran along the water, tracing the frame of the lake. The soldiers stared at the light glancing off its face—even the private, who should have been watching the road.

That day they passed one small village. It was only nine or ten houses, a couple of larger buildings, and a little jetty that hung calm and still on the water. No cars sat on the verge; no boats were tethered at the jetty. The only sign of human habitation—the first they'd seen since they left the mountain—was smoke rising from two chimneys. Glances flew around the truck. The smoke puffed, a steady stream of burnt-white.

Harker lifted a hand to touch softly at her bandages. This movement—this ginger graze at the site of her wound—seemed to remind them all why there were there, what their purpose was. The silence, and their journey, continued.

A while later the light began to slant over the fells. They

pulled over near a thinly wooded area close to the water's edge and made camp. It did not take long to set up their tents, to make a fire. Afterwards, the scout went to the water and stood unspeaking in contemplation of the valley, the smudge of forest, the darkening hills. Harker went to her tent. Daniel began to make dinner, the same combination of dehydrated rations and powders as they'd eaten the night before, but as he ripped open a sachet of dried soup, the private stood up.

I can't eat that stuff. Not again.

He grabbed his rifle and marched across the road, into the trees. Daniel watched him go. The scout looked at Daniel, shrugged, then turned back to the water, as if the lake and its ring of rising meadows held something for him that the others could not see.

Daniel sat feeding sticks into the fire. He was exhausted— partly due to their relentless travelling, partly to the poor night's sleep and partly to something else: a sense that things had gone too wrong to be righted. The fire grew higher. He began to feed it larger logs, to coax it into a state of embers. Suddenly he wanted to march into Harker's tent, to talk to her in a fast, loud voice about the bird, where they were going, why they were doing it, about the generals, about his parents' farm, about the woman she'd shot—but as soon as he pictured himself pulling at the zipper of her tent he realised how absurd the idea was, how he would never do something like that. A gust of failure swept through him, and for nearly a minute he fought back a choke of tears, until his turmoil was violently disturbed by the crack of gunfire.

Silence, then another burst of bullets. Soon afterwards

Daniel heard the heavy crunch of boots, and managed to wipe at his eyes and pull himself together before the private strode into the clearing. Something dark and ragged hung from his free hand. As he neared the fire, Daniel saw that it was a long-legged hare.

Dinner, said the private, shaking blood from the wet fur.

He sat down, pulled out his knife and began skinning the animal. He did it with ease, almost boredom. Daniel watched him underarm the hare's twisted guts into the trees. The private lifted the naked meat to his eye, then looked at Daniel, a question in his expression.

Daniel extended a palm.

Here. I'll cook it.

The private handed him the stringy corpse. It felt far too light to have recently been leaping through a forest. Daniel retrieved a small frying pan from their gear, and began to build a recipe in his head with the few ingredients they had: hare meat, salt, dehydrated peas. Moments later the scout returned from the lake, his eyes wide, as if he'd forgotten where he was.

When the hare was sizzling in the pan, Harker emerged from her tent, sniffing at the air. She looked at her soldiers, expressionless, then went back inside. Daniel felt the same sense of failure he'd battled earlier. But then she came back out with a small jar of dark liquid in her hand. She walked to the fire and poured a splash of it into the pan. Salt-tinged smoke rose into the air. Daniel and the other two soldiers leaned forward. They'd never seen this jar before, had no idea what Harker had done to their food. She could have poisoned them. But the smoke smelt so rich, so full of unknown flavour. Harker stowed the jar inside her jacket. Then she blinked at them, and it took them each a moment to realise that she was trying to give them a conspiratorial wink.

Daniel padded the meagre hare meat out with dried lentils and rice, and thanks to Harker's unknown seasoning the meal became the finest that any of them could remember eating. An alien savouriness bloomed on their tongues, at once gamey and delicate. It tasted, thought Daniel, like a chef had isolated the coppery flavour of blood and somehow rendered it delicious, if that were possible. All four scraped their plates clean and picked at the small bones. A sense of contentment rose between them, an unspoken wonder at the pleasure of the meal.

After they were done they washed their plates in the lake and returned to sit by the fire. Daniel assumed Harker would go straight to her tent, but instead she seemed happy to stay with them, crouching by the coals. The private threw a large fallen limb onto the low flames. The scout, who was shivering despite the fire, looked at the truck. After a moment of staring—as if he'd decided on a hard but correct course of action—he went to it and retrieved the heron's cage.

He sat it away from the fire, nearer the lake. With a deft movement, he pulled the oilcloth free from under his wrapped, knotted coat. Then, with cloth in hand, he went to his pack and fished out a few candles. He returned to the fire, ignoring how his comrades were watching him, and held one of the candles towards the coals while spreading the cloth over his knees.

As soon as the candle began to drip he held it over the cloth. Daniel realised he was aiming the dripping wax at the punctures the private's rifle had torn into the material that morning. The scout worked fast, shifting and turning the cloth in one hand, aiming the messy stream of wax with the other. It did not take him long to go through three candles. When he was done he stood and held the cloth out, inspecting his work. Wax now sealed all the bullet holes, creating glossy windows in the stiff, dark fabric.

The scout looked at them. When no one spoke or moved he gathered a breath and turned to the cage. He undid the knots in his coat, before sliding the cloth once again underneath it, feeling with his eyes closed, making sure it covered every inch of the bars. When he was satisfied he retrieved his coat and pulled it on. He returned to the fire, yanking his sleeves, buttoning his collar.

The cage sat there, once again black, still unmoving. A hum of anticipation rose in the air, although all four of them remained silent. The private lifted his feet off the ground. The fire lowered. Finally, Daniel spoke.

How did you know that would work?

The scout poked at the fire with a stick.

I didn't.

He stirred light into a dying coal.

It might not.

Daniel went back to looking at the cage, wondering what they'd do if something went wrong, if the bird escaped. He realised he was hoping that it would—that in a flash of damp anger it would explode through the damaged cloth and meld itself into the night-shining lake.

As he was imagining this, colour began to appear in the cage, visible through the small windows of wax. Pulses of blue light, flickering and shimmering, at times bright and loud, at others subtle and shaking, almost hesitant; a tiny aurora, playing under the cloth.

Perhaps, thought Daniel, the bird was trying to communicate with them. Or perhaps it was bored, or agitated, or experiencing an emotion they could not comprehend. Or maybe the bird was sleeping—maybe this show of restless colour was a projection of its dreams.

They watched the caged light dance through the wax. It was a long time before any of them went to their tents.

THE NEXT MORNING they left the lake behind and rose over the stone-rimmed fells onto a blond prairie. Feathered stalks of grass rose to waist height. Falcons plunged into this sea of grain, emerging with red fur in their talons. It was unbroken by forest or fence, and felt wilder than the farmland they'd seen earlier on the trip.

As they travelled, a smudge of colour began to rise on the horizon. At first Daniel thought it might be a low bank of storm clouds, but as they got closer it took on solidity, and colours of grey and black and green, and a uniform cragginess to its roof. Over the next hour it revealed itself as a low, long range of unbroken mountains, sitting unavoidably in their path.

The scout pointed at the range.

We go into the highlands. There's a plateau over the ridge.

At the base of the nearest peak the road began curling upwards, switchbacking along the face of the range. Large rocks gathered on the slope, held apart by copses of short, leafless trees. The going was slow as they twisted back and forth across the mountain, and the endless turning began to make Daniel feel sick. He looked backwards, down onto the plain of wild grass and the deep green valley beyond it, trying to settle his stomach by focusing on the unmoving horizon.

Below the sky, on the road they'd taken that morning, he could see a small black shape. It was too small to be a car, but it appeared to be moving like one. Daniel blinked. He kept twisting his neck back and forth as the truck curved up the range. The black shape disappeared, and he decided it must have been a far-off bird hanging in the air, perhaps one of the hunting falcons, its flight giving off the illusion of road travel.

Then he saw the shape again. It was still on the road, and it had moved closer, slightly closer. The truck turned yet again, and he swivelled his neck, and he felt sure that he would throw up, and then the road finally crested the top of the range, and the plains below were gone.

Their path levelled out on a high, colour-drained plateau. Daniel contemplated this new, rugged world though his window with half-sick wonder. The few scattered trees were even lower and thinner than they'd been on the ascent. Grey and teal dominated the land, extending in dull undulations to the bright-blue horizon in all directions. The world felt split open, splayed apart by the sky's clean reach.

The scout leaned out the window.

Nice country.

Nobody spoke in response. The landscape stayed like this as the road crawled slowly but gradually higher. Ragged rocks, leafless trunks, untamed tussocks of tough-looking grass. An occasional group of boulders, tumbled together at random. That night they camped beside one, employing the formation as a wind barrier. Daniel allowed an open fire, which they used to light the evening and heat their rehydrated food. This time, Harker did not offer her dark formula to the pan. He watched the night and blinked at the flames before falling into his tent, where he was netted by sleep.

The next morning he woke up strangely calm. He had slept well, and he had forgotten the black shape he'd seen on the road the previous day. Light was fuzzing across the ceiling of his tent. It was late, far later than he had slept in years. Not since his conscription could he remember being prone as the day broke.

Yet there he was, flat and tranquil as the sun burned high. He got up and left his tent, wringing out his sleeves, wiping his face with a dry sock. Water stood on the stalks of grass. The scout and private had the fire going again, were heating beans, no sign of hurry in their movements. Lieutenant Harker had packed her tent back into the truck, and was standing by the road doing the slow stretches she had once always done: legs, arms, back, neck, in practised succession, slow beauty in her limbs.

The familiarity of this image and the quietude of the camp reminded Daniel of all that he admired in his lieutenant. The misery and failure he'd felt beside the lake was gone, and the reverence he'd felt for Harker before their mountain mission returned and swelled within him. He waited for the lieutenant to finish her movements.

When she did, Daniel came to her side, not looking at her but instead studying the plain of rock and tussocks that ran from their feet to the horizon. When he spoke, he made sure he stayed out of her reach.

Feeling better?

She pulled at a toe, her ponytail brushing the rocky ground, and did not answer.

Are you still in pain?

Of course.

Can you at least let me look at it again? I might be able to help.

She stopped stretching. She looked up at the sky, then at the rocky land around them. After what felt to Daniel like a long time, she looked at him.

When I chose you for my squad, she said, I'd thought you'd be like this. I knew it, actually. I've always been a good judge of character.

At first, Daniel didn't know how to respond. He hadn't known she'd deliberately chosen him. He'd thought his assignation to her squad had been random. Eventually, he said: Like what? What do you mean?

Kind, she said. I thought my team needed a bit of kindness. It sounds stupid, I know. Others would have called it softness, even weakness. But I saw you there that day, huddled with all the other involuntary recruits, and I thought: there's a person who'll probably do the right thing, given the opportunity. And I thought that might come in handy, at some point.

She spoke airily, almost with detachment. As if he was only half-there, or only half-listening.

Again he didn't know what to think, what to say. So after a minute, he just said: Thank you.

A minute passed before he cleared his mind and spoke again.

Please. Let me look at your wound.

She resumed her stretching.

Why?

So you don't get infected. So we don't have to bury you somewhere up here, so we can deliver this...bird to the sanctuary. So we can complete our mission, lieutenant.

Harker pulled an arm across her chest.

What's the point?

He frowned.

The point? I only know what you told me. The generals

want it because they heard it existed, and they're in charge. Maybe they think it will make them look powerful. I don't care. I just want this to be over—

No.

She stretched her other arm.

What's the point in me getting better?

Before he could answer, she walked away.

ON THEY DROVE. The landscape did not vary from the rock and grass, occasionally dented by a lake or pond—patches of metallic water that looked like they had never held a current. Everywhere the sky was huge and wide. Its dusty-blue dome stretched further with each passing day. Clouds rarely fluffed by, and if they did they were small and insubstantial. Yet the nights still sang with rain. By morning the ground was drenched, the sky again empty.

This endless prairie of rock and sky began to unstitch Daniel's mind. The time they'd spent on the road became unclear to him, as did the distance they'd come. The days blended into each other. Clear skies gave way to dark rain, then returned as high blue fields. There were no towns—no houses or sheds or signs of human habitation. All that anchored him was the truck, his squad mates, the wax-pocked gleam of the bird's cage. It occurred to him that if it weren't for these reminders of his soldiering—if instead he were alone in this wide-skied, silent world—he might leave the hard comfort of the highway and stretch his legs out over the tussocks and boulders, the greys and beige greens, all the way to the edge of hazy blue.

During those hours in the truck he thought often of the day when Harker had recruited him. He tried to recall what he'd done when she'd walked past the row of medical students, asking questions about their studies, their families, their beliefs. But no matter how hard he strained, all he could remember was how scared he'd felt, how sure he'd been that he was about to die, how much he missed his parents and their green, tree-spotted fields.

He knew she'd lingered on him, that day. Her eyes had settled on his shaking face. But what she'd seen in him—some capacity for kindness—and what he'd said to her remained out of reach.

While he grasped at these memories, Lieutenant Harker did not speak. In her silence she made it easier for him to forget her wound, her unmaking. The scout and the private didn't talk to him either, or to each other unless they had to, but it was his lieutenant's lack of contact that had the strongest effect on him. Not fretting about her injury prevented him from castigating himself for his own behaviour, and further sent him out into the colours and textures of the plateau. Half-dreams dominated his thoughts. Nothing was good, and yet nothing got worse.

And just as it was Lieutenant Harker who had unchambered him, it was Lieutenant Harker who ripped him back down to the high earth.

They woke up one morning dry and cold—the first sign things had changed. Daniel, the scout and the private emerged from their tents and did not find the usual wet field of steaming puddles; instead they entered a world of whiteness, interrupted all over by flecks of familiar rock and grass. The light bounced into needles; the cold air clutched at skin. They blinked at the brightness and shivered in their jackets, before stepping with cautious awe out onto the snow.

The private found words first.

Is it meant to be like this? At this time of year?

I don't think so, said the scout.

He was rolling grains of snow into pellets, touching them against his cheeks.

Daniel huffed, turning crisp air into fog. He began walking in slow, vague circles, breaking the snow's contours with his boots, waiting for the delicious plunge that accompanied stepping into a drift of unknown depth. Around the camp he wandered, plumbing the length of his ankle, his shin, his knee, hunting the head swirl that came with each drop. Soon he hit the jackpot: a thigh-deep bank of snow. Down he sank, cold and fast, and that little bounce of vertigo came as a pure swipe across his mind, stripping away everything but giddy fear. Up he clambered and down he plunged: numb, empty, gasping.

Moisture clagged at his sock. He heard a zip—little metal teeth, tethering and untethering—and looked up to see that Lieutenant Harker had come out into this fresh scene. She began disassembling her tent. He ceased his antics and began picking his way towards her, stepping on pieces of revealed rock and frosted dirt. On his way he began pulling together what he was going to say, something to do with the weather, a question of whether it was due to the bird or the general unseasonality the country had been experiencing, but then he noticed the smell—a foulness in the chill.

It hooked into his nostrils. His eyes moistened and something bubbled in his throat. He looked down to see if his boot had disturbed something, but saw only snow and clean dirt. He had encountered plenty of snow, and it never smelt like this. Not in dancing flurries swirled by valley winds. Not in neat sheets that covered the slumber of winter fields. Not in yellow-brown banks beside boot-churned ditches, not in pinked slushes under bleeding limbs. These snows had only smelt like whatever had been mixed through their flakes, or like nothing at all.

Lieutenant Harker lurched around—a movement even more uncharacteristically awkward than usual—and he saw the river of viscous yellow pus coursing down her cheek from beneath her bandage. It ran free and slow, mixed with shining globs of blood, blood such a vivid scarlet it could have been healthy. Bitter knowledge burned in her eye, which was etched with broken bolts of red. She stumbled. Her infection fell to splatter the snow in thick, mustardy drops. Daniel felt the retch building in his neck. Above them, the sun burned bright and free in its field of blue.

WHEN HE TRIED to treat her, she didn't bother swinging a fist. She just pulled the gun from her holster. He expected her to hold it at her side—the sort of threat that would have ripped an insurgency to flapping tatters during the coup—but instead she pointed it straight at his head, in the same way she'd pointed it at the woman on the mountain.

We don't stop.

But—

No.

She looked at the scout. He and the private were watching the exchange from the road. When he noticed Harker's gaze he looked at his map, then at the sky.

If nothing slows us down, we'll reach the sanctuary this afternoon.

Then let's go.

Harker shoved the pistol back into its holster, missing on her first attempt. The order awakened the training in the private and the scout. They grabbed at their tents, flowing into routine.

Harker turned to Daniel.

One more day, she said. You can handle that.

The pus kept streaming down her cheek, her chin. Part of it rested on the jut of her lower lip, near the corner of her mouth.

Daniel felt like jumping into the rocks. He wanted to tear open the skin at the hollow of his neck.

It won't be one more day. We're days from anywhere you can get help. Weeks.

One more day.

That day passed differently to the previous ones. The world outside the truck did not deviate from its numb colours, its

190

bumpy plains, but its contours were marked all over by cushions of the bright-melting snow, which brought a gleam and glare to the once-muted landscape. Things changed inside the truck, too. The private still drove, the scout still fiddled with his map, but where Lieutenant Harker would usually have dozed she was restless, fidgeting, unsettled in every way possible. Again and again she raised her hand to her bandage. Each time she stopped, her hand shaking, before her fingers grazed its lemony crust.

Daniel became hyper-aware of Harker's movements. Soon that awareness transformed into a kind of heightened empathy. Her discomfort became his. He felt the needles of her frustration, her anger, her pain. They were so close. Less than a metre of air between them, air heavy with the rot of her wound.

When the smell of it defeated him—and it defeated him many times that day—Daniel made the private pull over, to let him splash the colours of his stomach onto the rock and snow. By early afternoon there was nothing but bile coming forth from within him: a foulness of his own.

Afterwards he stood hunched beside the truck, hands slipping down thighs, eyes bleary and drenched, throat and mouth burning. In those hunched moments, the relief he felt at having finished dragging up his stomach lining allowed him a small window of clarity. The effects of the days on the endless plateau, where his mind ran loose and idle, burned away. He could see the depth of his failure, the misery of their trip, the inevitable horror lying at the end of this day and perhaps every day that would come. He tried to imagine what they'd do once they were rid of the rain heron, but the past clogged his thoughts. His clarity was lost in the torture of the mountain woman, the flash of the bird's beak, the thump of Harker's bullet, the crack of her fist, the char of her antibiotics, the tributary of her infection. His farm came too, the bloating of the paddocks under rain, the stiff oil of a dirty fleece, the lilt of his parents' words without the words themselves reappearing in his mind. What he'd done in the coup. What he hadn't done. The sound of storms; the dampness of running rain. The clearing scent of pines. The sudden snow, stained a sick neon at his feet. At these moments, he felt sure that any future he found would be the same colour: a future of shining bile.

Nobody spoke until three o'clock, when the landscape finally shifted, after days of uniformity. A forest pushed through the rocks and loam. The trees were small, with pale trunks and thin branches that wore waxy blue leaves the shape of small ovals. Daniel stared through his sickness and recognised them as cider gums, and thought how strange it was to see them collected so tightly together. The road fed itself between their trunks, and as they drove through along it their world was dappled by the shadows that dropped from the ghostly trees. For half an hour they drove like this, covered in broken light, until the forest was split apart by a small road that swung off the highway, signalled by a faded, inscrutable signpost.

The scout pointed towards it.

Turn there.

The private swung the wheel, and the truck's tyres swapped asphalt for yellow gravel, although not for long. This new road was more of a driveway. It led into the trees, which clung tight to the road as it curled and bumped. After a few minutes they reached its end: a cattle grate, and beyond it a group of buildings, hemmed on all sides by the cider gums.

The gateless driveway ran through a low stone wall. Beyond it loomed the buildings, uneven in shape, height and structure. The private drove through and they came into a compound that made little sense. Sheds of corrugated iron. Some white-brick houses or admin blocks. High fences, built with ornate iron detailing—enclosures, perhaps. A large, concrete-walled structure with a domed roof of glass sat furthest back, against the gums. It all seemed randomly thrown together, with no central design or discernible layout.

No lights were on; nothing moved behind the fences, or beneath the curve of glass. The sanctuary was clearly still abandoned. The private let the truck come to a stop in a gravelled turning circle that sat in front of the nearest building.

Daniel waited. Beside him Harker mopped pus with a stained sleeve, flinching with each careful swipe, and he felt his pulse quicken, his throat squirm. He tried to imagine what they'd do when they had to turn around, and all he saw was the green splash of his bile. He supposed they'd keep driving, look for a general to report to. That might take them across the entire country, from one far border to the next. To the freezing south, to the hard heat of the north. Always hiding the bird. Always watching Harker deteriorate.

He wondered when she'd fire her gun again. Where she'd point it.

A banging sound intruded on his thoughts. Lieutenant Harker had stumbled out of the truck. She grabbed her pack and the cage, and began walking towards the lightless building.

The soldiers looked at each other, hesitating, before all three exited the vehicle. When they began to follow her, she stopped and turned.

Thank you for your work. You have carried out your orders. Now return to high command.

She turned again, kept stomping over the ground. It was ridiculous, perhaps suicidal. But at the sight of her retreating Daniel felt suddenly, deliriously free. They could leave. She might die, but they could leave. It was not a conscious thought, and he felt awful for thinking it, yet it filled him with a dark, weightless thrill.

There was a creak of metal on wood. A door opened. A figure came out of the building that Harker was approaching. The private walked back to the truck, his steps hurried and eager. The scout stared as Harker put the cage down and swayed on her feet, then he too returned to the truck, still staring at the cage, worry on his face. The figure from the sanctuary walked forward.

Daniel could hear Harker panting. Her back was to him, so he couldn't see her reaction as the stranger came closer to her. It was a man. He was young, wearing civilian clothes, and he had ruddy cheeks and soft, floppy hair. Words passed between him and Lieutenant Harker. The stranger had ignored the cage, and was reaching out to touch her face with a cloth he'd pulled from his coat. Daniel waited for her to strike him, waiting almost gleefully for her unpredictable wrath to fall on someone else.

But instead she swayed on her feet, before collapsing into his arms. The man caught her weight on his shoulder.

The scout and the private waited in the truck. Daniel

turned to join them. He was finding it hard to breathe, and for some reason he couldn't see properly. He wanted to get in the vehicle, to leave. He opened the door. But instead of climbing in he began gasping, and wiping at his eyes, and rummaging through his first-aid kit. Then he was marching towards the man his lieutenant had fallen onto.

As he approached, the stranger looked up at him, a fearful expression on his face. Daniel did not linger long enough to gain a true sense of the man. He just pushed the things he'd taken from his kit into this stranger's hand and rattled off some brief instructions. Then, without speaking to Lieutenant Harker, Daniel returned to the truck, climbed in, and told the private to drive.

BACK ON THE road, the scout consulted his map before announcing that the closest barracks was in the same direction they'd been going. Daniel felt a throb of relief.

Soon they had left the forest of cider gums behind. The plateau was again stark, open, bare. They drove with the windows down, and the fresh, snow-chilled air cleaned the smell of Harker's wound out of the truck. Daniel felt his stomach settle, his throat relax. He stretched out on the back seat. Every now and then he would instinctively look over his shoulder, checking on the cage that was no longer there, and every time he noted its absence he felt better. At dusk they found the first houses they'd seen on the plateau, clinging to the edge of a wide lake. They were large, lodge-like, probably fishing retreats for wealthy people who had liked to kill trout while holidaying.

They kicked in the door of the biggest house, found a feast of tinned fish and peaches, and slept in queen-sized beds. The night brought no rain. They woke to a snowless, smooth-stoned shore, the lake still and free of waves. Looking at the water, drinking a stolen cup of instant coffee, Daniel realised what he was going to do.

They got back in the truck and after an hour of driving they descended from the plateau into unremarkable, unworked farmland, much like the land they'd travelled through after first leaving the mountain. They reached a small town, where they found the barracks the scout had mentioned. When they reported to the commanding officer, Daniel informed him only of the vague outline of their mission, saying the details were classified. The private and scout went to bathe or eat while the officer made Daniel wait as he spoke to a colonel, or a general, or whoever he needed to. Three phone calls later he nodded at Daniel, who said something about needing a shower and left.

He walked past the bathrooms, past the mess, out into the parking area behind the barracks. There were no guards to stop him as he slid into the truck, twisted the keys the private had left in the ignition, and headed back onto the road.

He drove for four days. It would have only taken two, but he took back roads and detours, staying away from population centres, any places he thought might be hosting military or rebel presences. He ate dry rations, drank river water, slept in his tent. Occasionally he saw groups of people and vehicles clustered in the towns, but other than a few rocks thrown at his truck nobody bothered him, and he didn't initiate contact with anyone.

By the fourth day he reached a familiar valley. The road thinned. Swathes of green grass dominated the fields, and he was filled with relief. The stone-fruit trees held no fruit but looked sturdy and unmolested, and the fences seemed mostly intact. When he turned into the farm's driveway, he noted that the sign—which announced the name of the property in an ornate font—had been knocked down, but he didn't let it worry him; it had probably been the wind. He rumbled down the gravel, dodging the potholes and grooves that had not moved or changed. At the farmhouse the lights weren't on, but that was okay—it was not yet dark, and his parents didn't like to waste electricity. There were no cars, either, but they had probably taken them out into the fields, as they usually did while working.

He parked and walked across the small lawn in front of the house, the only piece of land that had not been put to use. Beyond it, over a fence, was an empty paddock. At this time of year it should have been filled with green feed crop, but he did not dwell on the thought. His parents were always rotating crops.

A shout from one of the fields broke the silence. He looked into the distance and saw two figures. They were too far away for him to make out who they were, what they were wearing, if they were men or women. They stood dark against the bare ground.

Daniel raised an arm. The figures ran towards him.

PART 4

WHEN I CLOSE my eye, I see her: the woman on the mountain. I used to see the northerner, but that was when I had both my eyes. Down my eyelids would fall, and down I'd see him go, thrashing, bleeding, the sucks and slaps of the tentacles dragging him under the reddened froth. I often grew angry that I wasn't seeing my aunt. Not in the moment she died, but in better times: those shivers of my childhood that were coloured bright by her laughter. But while I could summon memories of her, they only came with effort. And when my eyes inevitably closed, I always saw the northerner, and what I'd done to him.

Now he is gone from my darkness. When the rain heron plucked out my eye, it took that scene, too. These days, when I close my eye, I see the woman on the mountain. I see the fever in her skin. I see her broken in my arms. I see my bullet in her throat.

I CAN'T REMEMBER arriving at the sanctuary. If I concentrate I can see the shapes of trees, smell the rot of my infection, feel the slime of it on my cheek. But otherwise there is only shadow.

We woke up sometime later, the bird and I, in a large windowless room. I was lying on a medical cot, the kind found in doctors' surgeries. A door in the corner led to a shower and toilet. The walls were white and sterile, the floor badly polished concrete. I was still wearing my uniform. I remember feeling glad that I hadn't been undressed in my sleep, but angry that the uniform was still on me. I hadn't known how much I'd wanted to be rid of it until I woke up in that new place, still clad in its greens and browns, its muddy swirl. Mostly I felt groggy, disoriented. It took me a long time to remember where we'd been going—the destination we must have arrived at.

I looked around, glad to realise that the others were gone, especially Daniel. I couldn't have coped with any more of his concern, his troubled kindness. I don't know what I would have done if I'd had to spend another day watching him suffer in my presence.

My face had been washed, the bandage changed. Pus no longer leaked from my empty socket, which felt curiously dry. An itch in my forearm led me to a small fluff of cotton that had been taped over the skin. I'd been injected with something. Normally this would have annoyed me, but instead I felt loose, calm. I'd definitely been given some kind of painkiller, because the throb from my socket—which during the trip had been agonising, each bump in the road a fresh dagger—had dulled. I was aware of it, but it did not trouble me. I felt clean and fresh and rested. Once I swam out of my grogginess, I found that I had energy, and was hungry: two states I'd almost forgotten my body could enter.

In a corner of the room sat the heron's cage. I knew the bird was awake, because the edges of the cloth were moving, gusted about by puffs of moisture, and I could hear an occasional huffing. I watched the movement of the cloth, thought about the creature trapped beneath it. When I first saw the bird burst into its high grotto, when I watched its dance of wet light, I was mesmerised by it. Then it took my eye, and that feeling was replaced by terror, and with the terror came extraordinary pain, as I felt the icicle of its beak pierce the jellied rim of my eyeball. There's no other feeling like it—to experience the softest part of your exterior being stabbed and ruined is to know how vulnerable you really are. As fast as my eye was skewered, it was ripped out. Blood sprang, and for the briefest of moments I could feel a coldness, a breeze at the back of my eyeball. I know it didn't happen, I know it was a phantom pain, but I can still remember it: the night air licking at the back of my eye.

You would assume that as soon as it left my body, the eye went dark. And I'm sure it did—of course it did—but all the same, I have memories of witnessing myself from its new perspective, threaded onto the heron's beak. From up there, I could see the bleeding, screaming cyclops I had become. Then that vision begins turning, twisting, and I see myself flashing in and out of frame, as the bird tosses my eye off the tip of its beak in a neat arc, before catching it in its open mouth.

That's what my men never knew. The bird didn't just take my eye—it ate it. Down the river of its throat my stolen sight coursed, and as it was squeezed and swallowed I witnessed the eye's path, a darkening current, the high stars growing fainter through the closing beak, until it settled in the bob of a lightless lake, and I saw no more.

My eye went out, and the only view I had left was the one I still have: single-orbed and depthless. The oilcloth was thrown over the bird, and the creature was hidden from me. There in that foreign room, in a different high place, I realised how hidden it had stayed. I hadn't seen a feather of it since it devoured my grace.

EVENTUALLY THE DOOR was knocked upon, and a man entered the room. He came in backwards, using his hip to nudge the door open, carrying a tray of food with both hands. Without speaking, he walked to my bed and placed it on a small table near my pillow. When his hands left the tray he finally turned to me—clean cheeks, floppy hair, neutral expression— and I remembered how I had collapsed onto him. I remembered how my knees buckled, how my weight had been propped against his body. He had held me gently, with no awkwardness, even as I had smeared my infection all over his shoulder. I didn't remember him doing anything but standing there, holding me, until I found some strength in my legs and the curl of his fingers had led me inside.

Now those fingers weaved together, his hands a nest, as he stood before my bed. I sat up and rubbed my arm.

Good morning, he said. I'm Alec.

Did you give me an injection?

Yes.

What was it?

I don't know.

He shrugged.

Your friend—I mean, one of your troops—gave it to me when you arrived. He said I needed to administer it while you were sleeping, and that you needed to rest.

Daniel jumped into my mind. My medic, pleading to help me, as I refused to let him near. I was suddenly, furiously angry. Then I thought of him swabbing at my socket by the bank of a river, the night after I'd lost my eye. I thought of how I'd struck him at the stone farmhouse. I remembered the sobs I'd heard leak from him that night by the lake—tiny, hopeless sounds, just loud enough to reach me in my tent.

I felt myself cool. I looked back at this Alec person.

Don't ever touch me again.

If you say so.

He left my bedside, walked to the door. At the cage, he stopped.

What's in here?

You haven't looked?

He looked at me, his face placid.

It's yours. I didn't think I should look without your permission.

Scepticism must have shown on my face, because he smiled. I realised he wasn't lying. If he had looked, he wouldn't be this calm. I motioned at the cage.

Go on.

He knelt down. As his fingers moved towards it the cloth flared up, and fog lifted from the gap. He recoiled, and glanced at me, confusion on his round face. I kept my expression still. He turned back and dipped a finger below the edge of the fabric. I saw the apprehensiveness in his posture—hands yanked back to his chest. The cloth settled. Slowly he regrasped it, and then carefully, with tentative fingers, he peeled it away from the bars. The aperture he created was obscured by his back; I couldn't see what he was seeing. He had stopped breathing. I held my own breath, made sure I was not moving; I gave myself every chance to hear the swell of his lungs. But still I heard nothing. His shoulders and back were raised high. Nothing came from the gap he'd created in the cloth—no fog or ice, no burst of sound or bird.

At last he let go of the cloth and stood up. I waited for the questions, the incomprehension. But he just stood there, not asking anything, not even turning towards me. He rubbed at his arms, his neck. After half a minute he took a step towards the door.

Wait, I called.

He paused, his hand resting on the doorknob.

You must have somewhere better for it than here.

I could see the agitation twitching in him. Then he pivoted, grabbed the cage's handle and swung it through the door. His body followed, disappearing behind the click of the closing latch as he left me to lie in that strange bright room alone.

IT'S NOT THAT I wanted to die. I just couldn't see the point in continuing to live. I had done the world nothing but ill. I wasn't as bad as some, and during the coup I had tried to avoid causing unnecessary suffering, but I had known for a long time how my skills and inclinations were being used against others. I had ignored it, rationalised it, even played it to my advantage. But after what I did on the mountain—my greatest cruelty, in the midst of what was perhaps my greatest success—I realised that unless I changed, I would continue to make life worse for all those I was loosed upon.

After shooting the woman, I tried to think about my own life with logic and detachment. What I should do, how I should act, now that it had been incontrovertibly confirmed that I was a force of illness. I knew the generals wouldn't allow me to change. If anything, I would be made to become worse. I thought that maybe I'd maim my leg. One leg, one eye—surely they'd release a soldier that broken.

But I knew they wouldn't. Not now that I'd brought a myth to life.

I was in a lot of pain as I considered these things, so I kept closing my eye, which meant I kept seeing the mountain woman. Again and again I saw her break and bleed and fall. Completing missions, taking pills, drinking clean water, watching the sun climb and the clouds run—it all stopped making sense.

If I'd had any courage, I would have nosed the northerner's pistol into my socket and fired it for a second time. But I have never been brave. Just strong, and at times—too many times—cruel.

THE MORNING AFTER I told the man named Alec to take the bird, I woke up clear-headed and without pain. I rose at something like dawn, drank some water, brushed my teeth, and was doing my stretches before I remembered the bird, my eye, the woman I'd shot. I showered. I found some stiff, block-coloured hiking clothes in a cupboard and left the room.

Through the door there was a short corridor, and at the end of that another door that led outside. Fog hung thick and moist, right down to the ground. I could only see a few metres past my hands. I stepped out onto a path, into the mist, and let the contours of the trail guide me wherever they went.

I could occasionally make out the trees that hemmed the compound. Through gaps in the fog their brown-white trunks loomed, always appearing closer or more distant than they had first seemed. Or maybe that was just another symptom of the death of my depth perception. Much closer than the trees were the buildings of the sanctuary. Small, flat-roofed things, not very different to the barracks I was used to. They looked like offices and accommodation, but I didn't enter any of them to investigate. In my two-eyed life I would've scouted them, found their exits, their points of strategic interest or value, but in my newly adjusted state they were too boring to bother with. I could imagine what was inside them: single beds, flatpack desks, flip calendars, green lamps, ancient filing cabinets; beige dread.

More interesting were the empty enclosures scattered between the buildings. Barred cages, topped in spikes, rendered useless by gates that gaped wide and loose. Inside were the remnants of artificial environments—hollow logs, rocks assembled into climbable structures, the thirsty dents of empty cement ponds. Gravel neatly scraped into tiny yards, unmarred by footprints. Dry branches stretched out at head height, supported by lattices or chains. It was an abandoned zoo, or a rehabilitation clinic, or a place of protection for endangered animals. Perhaps it really was a sanctuary, or once had been.

I found the outer gate where we'd arrived, and the spot where I'd fallen onto Alec. I turned back into the compound, and saw that the fog was thinning. More of the forest was visible from here, and so was the only structure of any size: a cathedral-like building three times the size of the others, with a domed glass roof. I went straight towards it, stepping on rock, slipping on frost, ignoring the paths.

An unlocked door led into a narrow room. Two rows of floor-bolted stadium chairs were arrayed before an enormous window that also served as a wall between this corridor and the rest of the building. Alec was sitting in the centre of the front row. He looked up as I entered the room. His hair still flopped at odd angles, and his posture was bad. For a second, I wanted him to straighten up—I wanted to jam my palm into the small of his back. I took a seat, leaving an empty one between us. He spoke first.

Good morning.

Morning.

How are you feeling?

Fine. Better. Fine.

I was annoyed at the question, annoyed at the unneces-sary tripling of my response, and was ready to snap something at him. But he said nothing. He kept looking at the window, hunched forward, back bent. I realised I was watching him, so

I stopped, and copied him in looking straight ahead.

Through the glass I could see an exaggerated version of the abandoned enclosures I'd spent the morning exploring— long branches, fake structures, ropes and chains, and swinging apparatus of metal and wood and bone. The floor was covered in decaying leaves and artificial ponds, although these cement indentations were full, connected by unmoving streams. It looked less neglected than the others. High at the top I saw the clear dome, its thick glass, the white banks of mist bobbing at its outer surface. Alec's voice appeared, almost as a whisper.

It's remarkable.

I didn't answer. The enclosure was impressive in its way, I supposed, but it was empty. Suddenly he stopped breathing again, the way he had in my room the day before. I glanced at him and saw a wide wetness in his eyes. I looked back at the enclosure.

I hadn't seen it at first because it hadn't been there—not as itself, or the self I had seen in the mountain grotto. Now I saw it rise from the sad fake pond, as I had seen it rise from the mountain pool. Up from the water it formed, flying on blue-wet wings, glistening into being as it made for a chain-suspended branch. It came to a brief perch, then leapt to a hanging tyre on the other side of the aviary. In its path between perches it flapped, soared, and briefly burst into a shower of rain, before reforming in the moment it landed. There its beak fell into its wing, preening back and forth, straightening feathers, shedding streams of water, wet-shining and ghostly.

Seeing it again produced no great reaction in me. No bubbles of terror, no horrible memories. I just watched it, as amazed as I had been when I saw it on the mountain. After a while I closed my eye, half-hoping that my lost one would open inside the bird, revealing to me the swishing wetness of its belly. But all I saw, as usual, was the mountain woman, this time shovelling blackberries into her mouth as I watched from the shadow of a pine.

I opened my eye and saw a cloud parting overhead, brightening the aviary. The bird twisted its head upwards, then dissolved into a bank of rising fog. It lifted past the winding boughs of dead wood, the dirty-white walls, towards the curve of glass that was letting in the sunlight. A metre below that high window the mist-bird reformed into a spray of dense droplets, which hung in the air for a heavy second before shooting up to smack against the glass. I could hear the angry pelt of them on the pane. When they had all smashed into their target they fell again, shattered into drops that dispersed again into mist, then again into hard drops, which again flew like wet bullets into the window. The glass did not shake, did not grow hairlines. The drops broke, fell, reformed, and shot again.

After this third attack the water stopped falling. It stayed on the glass in a smeared puddle. I watched it glisten, watched it change again into steamy condensation that clung to the glass like breath. From the ground, I couldn't tell how hot that moisture was, if it was hot enough to weaken the window. I wasn't sure how hot I wanted it to be, if I was on the side of any particular outcome.

I've always liked animals, Alec said. I used to catch them and bring them home. I'd dam crabs into rock pools at the beach, then scoop them into a bucket filled with sea water. Or

I'd trap skinks behind books and tumble them into my palms. Back at our house I'd put the crabs in the bath, where they died, and the skinks in my bedroom, where they escaped through the crack under the door, or the windows I kept leaving open. When I did manage to keep them alive or in one place, my mother would inevitably find them and let them go. She liked animals too, but not as much as I did. Maybe she liked them more when she was younger; most people like things more intensely as children, I guess. Although I don't know what she was like as a child.

All I know is that when I was a child—he pointed at the condensation still heating the glass dome—I believed rain herons were real. I believed everything I was told. What child doesn't? It wasn't until much later that, like everyone else, I understood that they were made up. An old story about droughts, luck and cruelty. I wanted to believe in a bird made of water, as harsh as it was generous, but I was taught it was impossible. I limited myself to crabs and skinks. Birds made of flesh and feathers. Then the coup happened, and the world stopped making sense—to me, and to everyone. And now you appear with something that I had convinced myself didn't exist.

He pointed again at the condensation. It was changing shape, changing temperature. Instead of turning into mist or rain it was falling slowly, creeping and hardening into mottled, sharp stalactites tethered to the glass by anchors of bristle-patterned frost. The air took on a chill. I began to shiver.

I wish you hadn't brought it here.

There was no accusation in his voice. No anger. Just regret and sorrow.

I didn't know what to say. Mentioning orders or missions suddenly felt like the most childish justifications imaginable, so I said nothing.

He saw me shivering and took off his coat. I thought he was going to hand it to me or, worse, drape it over my shoulders. But he just put it on the chair between us, an act both obvious and subtle, and said in the same sad voice: I suppose we should tell Gladstone and Ramiro.

FROM THE FIRST, he was gentle like that. Not in a way that communicated sympathy, or concern, or confusion. He was just gentle. Quiet, with no skein of violence running beneath that quietness. He didn't admire me. He didn't fear me. He didn't love me. He didn't regard me as anything other than a wounded stray, a stranger who needed to be taken care of. And that's what he did. With quiet force, he took care of me.

IN A GAP in the trees, behind the drear of the abandoned compound, was a kind of garden. Tussock grass had been herded into a humpy lawn, bisected by a roughly gravelled path. At its end the cider gums strained upwards, towards light. Beside the trees was a patch of grassless dirt, and on it sat a grey, humped boulder. Scraped into its face, above the disturbed earth, were two words: *Gladstone* and *Ramiro*.

I found them when I first came here, said Alec. But not like this.

He had brought me to these graves after we left the aviary. It was a short walk, and the fog had mostly lifted.

After a breath, he continued.

When I arrived they weren't in this spot. There had been a blizzard. Unexpected, out of season. They weren't prepared. I experienced a mild version of it on my drive up, and by the time I got here most of the snow had melted, but still—it was the middle of summer. It didn't make sense.

I found them in their quarters, sitting next to an empty gas heater. Two of their windows had been broken—tree limbs, I suppose. Or wind. Blizzard wind. They were huddled against each other, their backs to a wall. I had to use a hammer to peel a frozen blanket away from their bodies. They were holding hands. They weren't a couple, not that I knew of—just scientists working alongside each other. But the cold had fused the skin of their palms and fingers together. I couldn't prise them apart, although I suppose I didn't try very hard. When the rest of the snow melted and the soil thawed I buried them here. I sent a report, never heard anything back. That was six months ago.

He said this in a rush, as if he'd been waiting to get it out all at once. It was the first time I'd seen him do anything in a hurry. When he was done he kicked some gravel from the grass onto the plot.

What were they doing up here?

He fiddled with the hem of his jacket.

I have no idea. Something with animals, I suppose. This is a wildlife sanctuary, or it was. Although there were no animals when I got here, not even any corpses of ones killed by the blizzard. They might have been preparing the place for new arrivals. Or maybe they were researching the climate or weather patterns. That's what makes the most sense to me, and it's what I want to believe. If they were up here trying to figure out why the seasons have become so unpredictable, then their deaths meant something. But now...

He looked at me, then back at the aviary.

I have to assume they were waiting for the heron. For you.

The wind had picked up, carrying almost all of the fog away, revealing the muted colours of the trees. I met his eyes.

And you. Why are you here?

He turned and began walking back towards the compound. I went with him. I thought he wasn't going to answer me, but then more words rushed out of him.

I was a hopeless soldier, he said. Absolutely terrible. I hesitated all the time; I hated firing guns; I couldn't remember formations or procedures. The simplest orders confused me. I was involved in two deployments before my captain demanded I be transferred. They tried to move me to another squad, but none of the others wanted me. I served on one more mission and performed badly, even worse than on my first two, and afterwards I was ordered back to barracks. I was bumped around desk jobs, doing administration, typing up memos, that sort of thing, although that didn't come naturally to me either. I kept misspelling orders, putting the wrong officers' names on briefings. Eventually I was told that I was no longer a private—I was a research assistant. I was given a car, and told to report to my new commanding officers at this sanctuary. I didn't know I was coming here to bury them.

We were treading past an enclosure filled with empty ponds and black dirt. I usually hated conversations, had hated them even more since losing an eye. But for the first time since my wounding I was not in pain. I was not cold or hot, not hungry or angry. Just hollow—riddled out, scraped raw.

Why did you stay?

After I reported the deaths of Gladstone and Ramiro, I waited for a message on the radio. It's the only thing that works up here. What will they do with me now? I remember thinking. Where will they send me next? I waited and waited. No response came, so I started walking the old trails that cut across the plateau. Late each afternoon I came back to the sanctuary, checked the messages, and would always find nothing. I started taking longer walks. I explored the forest; I crossed the grasslands; I slept under the clearest, cleanest skies I've ever seen. Have you ever seen as many stars as you do up here? They're not easy to leave.

The longer I went without receiving any orders, the more I didn't want to return. What would I do down there? I was a terrible soldier. I didn't even want to be one; I never had. I'd only signed up because I was furious with my mother. I realised

I could stay up here, and as long as they didn't contact me, I wasn't disobeying any orders. It wasn't desertion; I couldn't be punished for it. There's enough dried food here to last years. I could catch trout in the streams; I could maybe snare a rabbit or two. The coup would go on, or it wouldn't. The world didn't need me, and up here I needed only the world. Not the people in it.

My response came unbidden, instinctively.

You talk about her a lot.

Who?

Your mother.

What?

Lines appeared in his face.

I don't think I do. And if I do, it's an accident. I haven't spoken to anyone in months.

He stopped walking. We were nearing the middle of the compound.

What about you? Why did you stay?

I just got here.

But surely you have other places to be. Your wound is going to heal and you've completed your mission, as far as I can tell. There must be things they want you to do. Places they want you to be.

How would you know?

I wouldn't. But I know who you are.

He started walking away, fast, the sort of walk that isn't designed to be followed.

I may be a bad soldier, he called over his shoulder, his voice cut by the wind. But I'm not a blind one. Not even half-blind.

219

I stood still, watching him march, waiting to feel furious. But I felt no anger. I just wondered what it meant, him knowing who I was, and what he thought of me.

And besides, he yelled again, before he marched his voice out of range. What else is worth talking about, if not our mothers?

HE WAS RIGHT, of course. I had no real reason to stay. But that night, as I lay in my starchy sheets, I didn't think about that. The other events of that day revolved in my mind. I couldn't settle or concentrate on one thing. The deserted buildings. The enclosures devoid of life. Alec. The melting, shifting, misting creature I'd brought to his huge cage, and his sorrow that I'd brought it to him. The frozen scientists who had probably been waiting for it. Alec's rush of words, his loneliness, his mother. His flash of emotion when I pointed out his repetition of her. My thoughts circled on his story, and ran it alongside memories of my own. His failure in the military; my awful success. I traced my khaki-clad accomplishments backwards, back and back, until I was there on my cold coast, shaking and numb, holding the northerner's pistol. Everything swirled, and my head ached, until I closed my eye, and the mountain woman chased me into sleep.

THE NEXT MORNING I found him at the aviary again. He was sitting on the same seat. When I entered the building I saw a flash in the corner of my eye, through the glass. I looked into the enclosure just in time to see the bird disappear into the pool of water. I sat down, again keeping a spare seat between us.

I supposed he would start talking again. About himself, the bird, his mother, how he'd recognised me. I waited for his words to tumble out, not knowing how I'd respond, if I'd respond at all. But he just sat, sipping at a steaming thermos, staring through the glass. Waves had begun dancing on the surface of the water—small sets that rose on the far side, ran and built across the pool, to fall in small heaves on the concrete shore closest to us. I realised that I wanted him to speak; I wanted to hear his voice again, whatever he spoke about. But even after half an hour, he said nothing. It was as if all the words he'd spilled out the day before had exhausted him, and he needed to replenish his reserves. He offered me the thermos, which sent warmth deep into the flesh of my fingers and palm as I gripped it, sitting still, watching the little waves rise and die.

IN THE DAYS that followed I expected to wake up each morning brimming with purpose and vigour, with a plan to leave, to take his car, to return to the only thing I was good at. But morning after morning, it didn't happen. I would wake feeling hollowed and light. The thought of leaving, even making a report, brought great thumps of nausea. It took me a while to realise that, along with my eye, I'd lost a fixed point of who I was, and what it was about me that mattered.

It was around this time that I also realised that I wanted to go on living.

Instead of the things I would have done had I been my earlier self, I took to joining Alec on his walks. After breakfast, the highland sun still low, I'd follow him on one of the many paths that cut through the gums. Over dirt and duckboards we'd tread, until we reached the edge of the cider-gum forest and were spat out onto the rocky, mossy plains of the plateau. From there Alec would pick out less obvious routes amid the rocks and creeks and tarns, signalled only by carefully piled cairns. We'd walk for hours, sustained by the nuts he kept in a small pack, the forest growing smaller in the distance behind us. There was so much more water out there than I had expected. The ground was full of it, in puddles, bright snowdrifts, ever-soaked mud. It was hard to find dry places to put my feet, but I had my leather boots, so the squelch of each step did not reach my skin.

Amid all this water were tussocks, heather, moss, a palette of muted greys and greens that revealed more texture and colour each time I ventured out into it. Occasionally highland flowers sprang up, white or purple-petalled, thin-stemmed. Streams joined the soggy landscape together, some brown with tannin, others steely, others the grey of rain and rock. They fed into small lakes, which we skirted, circled, ate beside. The first time we sat down for lunch I looked out over the lake we'd found—small, still, almost a pond—and watched the tiny, agitated birds that flitted from rock to sedge to stem. They were the only creatures I saw during my whole time up there. Alec told me he'd seen small bushy-cheeked mice, and something that had looked like a ferret or quoll, but all I saw were those miniature birds that seemed too fast for this world.

We talked, more and more with each expedition. Not about ourselves, or our circumstances, or the strangeness and awfulness of what had brought us together. Instead we edged around subjects that people spoke about before the coup—books, films, foreign places—as well as what we knew about the land we were travelling through, which only extended as far as what we were seeing. I came to realise that Alec actually knew very little about the plateau, only marginally more than I did, but his mesmerisation had led him to cross almost every inch of it. It was an obsession that felt, at times, contagious.

We didn't always walk out onto that wet, ragged plain. Sometimes we jumped into his vehicle—a dual-cab utility with a large tray—and travelled to climb the bare peaks that sprang from the plateau, or to the high crags of the range that marked the edge of the highlands. These climbs weren't technically challenging, or even all that dangerous, but we had to help each other over the higher ledges. On these ascents I was keenly aware of my adjusted sight, and the deficiencies in my balance. At times I felt uncontrollably vulnerable, and I only managed to make it up each peak with Alec's help. He had a soft grip, and he wasn't notably strong, but he was there, each time I wobbled or gasped or felt my knees tip and my head lurch. At the top we would pause on these hard ceilings of the world, looking out over the high plain that stretched below us, reaching in all directions to the cloud-heavy horizon, before finding our way back to the car, and then to the shelter of the sanctuary.

Some days—rainy days, cold days, days of snow or darkness—we didn't walk at all. On mornings like that I lay in bed, or braved the weather to tidy the area around the grave of Gladstone and Ramiro. I had no reason to do it, but on our walks, and in the hours of night, I often thought about them, and saw them in the way Alec had described them, dying in each other's grip, their palms glued together. I'd think of them underground, composting into each other, and keeping their plot clean somehow became an important thing to do.

But that took only minutes. We spent most of our time in the inclement weather in the aviary, watching the bird morph and preen, disappear and reappear. On one of these viewings, perhaps a week after I'd arrived, Alec's words finally came back to him.

I hit her.

I looked at him, twisting my neck in the way I now had to.

My mother, he said. I hit her.

He was leaning forward, staring at the floor.

Why?

He took a breath.

Remember how I told you I liked animals?

He gestured at the aviary.

I always preferred them to people. I struggled to make

225

friends. The crabs, the lizards, any little bird I could find—I found infinite pockets of time to spend with them. We were similar in that way. Great with animals, terrible with humans. So when the troubles started, when the seasons broke, when the jobs disappeared and blame began being thrown in every direction, my mother ignored it all, and told me to, as well. There's nothing we can do that'll change things, she would say. But I didn't like that. Even though I was no good with people, I wanted to help. She wouldn't listen to me. I was a petulant, shouting teenager. I don't really blame her.

I was mad at her, all of the time. The country was falling to pieces—at least, our part of the country was. My school had been closed for six months. People were breaking into shops, robbing pensioners. I was so furious, but my fury had no direction, and she wasn't doing anything about it. She wasn't doing anything at all. I had no father, no brothers or sisters, no other family. And my mother just kept on keeping to herself. Closing the curtains, drinking cheap wine. I would yell at her, and she'd either ignore me or tell me I didn't understand, that there was nothing we could do, that we were best off keeping our heads down and letting people be people. I'd shout, she'd roll her eyes, and outside someone would be beaten and windows would be smashed.

One afternoon I was walking home from a rally, one of the rare peaceful ones. I passed a cove I knew well. I'd swum and played there my whole life. To me it was a place synonymous with happiness and safety. Only this time, as I walked, I saw four men standing thigh deep in the water. They were carrying poles and splashing about. I stopped, trying to figure out what they were doing. I wish I hadn't. A grey rubbery slope pushed out of the water, followed by a spray of mist. It was a dolphin. I saw how slowly it was swimming, how laboured its movements were, and that's when I saw that the water around it held patches of pink. The men had it cornered in the cove, and the lengths of wood they carried were not poles but spears or pikes. I watched them stab the dolphin, watched the points pierce and hook into that grey mound of skin.

They were hungry, I guess. Most people were. But even so—it was a dolphin. I ran into the water, began shouting. I don't know what I said. They ignored me at first, but eventually two of them broke off their attack and came towards me. They ignored my insults. They didn't even really look at me. They just shook their pikes, and when I didn't back away they dropped them in the water—I remember watching them float—before one of them held my arms while the other hit me.

When they were done they threw me on the shore. I passed out for a while. I remember hearing the sound of something heavy being dragged over the beach, and the beep of a truck reversing. When I came to fully, the men and the dolphin were gone. The only sign of them was a furrow in the sand, and the pink tinge of the tide.

When I got home my mother ran to me, asking what had happened. I didn't lie. I was sure I had done the right thing, but she became furious and began berating me. I was trying to help, I told her, but she said I hadn't helped anyone, that I was lucky not to have been killed. I got angry. I started shouting. She called me a fool. The next thing I knew she was on the floor, holding her face as my hand hurt.

I can't remember the details of what happened next very

clearly. It's hard for me to think about, even now. But I know it felt like I was standing there for a long time, and she was lying there for a long time, holding her mouth. It can only have lasted a few seconds, but the memory feels like thirty minutes, an hour. Then what I'd done overwhelmed me, and I started crying and shouting, I don't know what, and then I left. I ran outside. She said something to me, but I wasn't paying her any attention as I ran for the door.

I went back, later, far too late. By then I'd finished my training, and was about to be sent on my first mission—the first of my many failures. But she wasn't there. Her car was gone; the house was empty. I haven't seen her since. I still don't know where she is, or if she's alive. And no matter how hard I press my memory, I can't recall what she said to me as I left her lying on the carpet with a mouthful of blood.

Alec looked exhausted, as if the revelation had sapped a lot of energy.

He must have kept this quiet for a long time, I thought. Or perhaps he'd never spoken about it at all, or even thought about it, if he could help it. I didn't know what to say, if he wanted me to say anything. I could feel the space around us expanding to accommodate what I would say. And while I had not just one thing to say but many, too many to keep living with, my flesh seized up, and all I could get out was that my mother had died when I was a child.

He said he was sorry that I'd gone through that, and I told him it was okay. We spent the rest of the afternoon watching the rain hit the aviary roof, until we became hungry enough to hurry through the falling water towards the kitchen.

I WENT TO him that night. His bed wasn't hard to find. I just walked outside and found light glowing through a window of the smallest building in the sanctuary, set back against the cliffs. I stomped through the cold, opened the door, and found a room even sparser than my own. A concrete floor. A lamp. A sink. A table with a single chair. A narrow bed, holding Alec, a book cracked open in his fingers.

I had expected him to be gentle, yielding. But from the moment I came to his bed, pulling off my clothes, not speaking, he moved up and grabbed at me with as much force and hunger as I did at him. We were clumsy, and there wasn't enough room in the little bed, but soon we stopped noticing the banging of our elbows and the squeeze of our hips as we rolled and repositioned. Soon a rhythm developed that took me out of that room, and I was grabbing at him harder, moving faster, putting my lips and teeth to his skin, saying things I can't remember.

It had been a long time. A whole year, maybe longer, and then it had only ever been with people I'd barely known. Men I'd been attracted to in the brief times of quiet during the coup—never other soldiers. Civilians who were just as willing as I was to make our time together urgent, transactional. Never anything that would last, never with anyone I wanted to see again.

So at first, that night with Alec, it felt strange to be touched, as if my body was rediscovering something that had been lying dormant under my skin. Afterwards, in that tiny bed, our skin stayed together. His arms circled my shoulders, his hands resting on my back, while my cheek pressed at his chest and my knuckles pushed into his thighs. He dozed off, and his even breathing was the only sound I could hear. I leaned into his warmth and tried to go to sleep. I inched towards his body, closed my eye, and when I did I didn't see the woman on the mountain. I saw only darkness, a high quilt of stars, and him.

THE NEXT DAY we walked again out onto the plateau, our skin marked all over by the night. The sky was free of clouds and the air was cold and scentless. Everywhere the land glistened with moisture. The rocks and grass and pools spread out before us in a patchwork of grey-green-blue-brown so vivid I wanted it painted, photographed, turned into something more than a memory, something physical that I could take with me.

When we stopped for lunch I realised why I was thinking like this, finding ways to remember this place: I was going to leave. It hadn't been a conscious decision, but as soon as it hit I also knew where I was going to go and what I was going to do. It must have been percolating inside me, growing in strength without revealing itself, until now.

I looked at Alec. He was chewing some nuts, staring at the lake we were sitting beside. I was going to tell him that I was leaving, but I was swamped by the memory of everything he'd told me the day before, and how I'd said nothing. I wondered what he would do when he knew I was abandoning him, and I didn't know how to tell him, what to say, and as he felt my eye on him he turned towards me, and suddenly I was talking.

I'm sorry about what happened with your mother, I said. And I'm sorry I didn't have anything better to say than that mine was dead, which is true, but it's not all of it.

I meant to stop there, to pause and gather my thoughts, but instead my words kept tumbling out.

Things happened before, I said. I thought I was right but I wasn't. I wasn't justified; I wasn't the lesser of multiple evils; I was just cruel and wrong. And before that, long before—I've been wrong for a long time. When I said my mother died I wasn't lying, but I had an aunt. And there was a man from the north. He was so stubborn; he was one of those men who feels entitled to something because he knows it exists, the way the generals are about that bird, and the winter was so much colder than it should have been, and people should know how to swim, right? Can you? Everyone can. Do you know how much water can fit in a throat? Do you know how much blood runs in a body? By the time I reached the mountain—that's where the bird was—I thought I was a different person, but I wasn't; I never really changed, and...

At that point my words began running into one another. I was out of breath, and a cold sheen of sweat had coated my face, but I tried to keep telling him what I had done. I didn't care: I wanted him to know everything. My throat hurt, and I felt dizzy. Eventually I stopped trying to talk. I became aware of his hand on my back, resting light as fog.

It's all right.

I'm trying to tell you—

It's fine.

He gripped down on my shoulder.

There'll be time.

I began to get my breathing under control. I took a slug of water from the bottle he offered me, before standing up.

I need to walk.

Okay.

On the way back I pulled myself together and told him that I was leaving, that I was taking the bird back to the mountain where I'd captured it. I said I'd done terrible things there, and the people who lived there would probably kill me if they got a chance, but I was going anyway.

He listened, and kept walking, and whistled at the possibility of my death. He only spoke when I was finished. And of all the things I'd said, both on the walk and back at the lake, he seemed most concerned about transport.

I guess you'll need my car.

I stared at him.

I suppose so.

Not sure if you should be driving in your condition.

I can drive.

Sure?

I don't need your help.

I think I'll come anyway.

We continued on, and didn't speak again. But something took hold within me, something bigger and stranger than the world around us. I reached for his hand. A feeling of slowness came over me. In the cool air, my body was ringed by warmth.

AS THE SANCTUARY came into sight we were treading duck-boards, stretching hamstrings over remnants of the rain, and the narrowness of the path and the wide expanse of the puddles meant our legs and hips kept knocking against each other. As we edged around a particularly large pool Alec stumbled and leaned on me, his shoulder pressing into my chest, his arm landing on my collarbone. This contact hauled me back to the night, our heated weight, and I wanted him again. He stayed pressed against me for longer than was necessary, so I knew he felt it too.

We began to walk faster. Soon we came back into the compound, through the trees, and all I was thinking of was pulling him to me. Maybe it was this desire that distracted me, that prevented me from noticing what I might otherwise have seen. Or maybe it was just how I was now. The old me would have noticed instantly that something was wrong. I would have seen how the gravel had shifted in the driveway, or how the grass had been flattened into a faint line that led behind one of the abandoned enclosures. I would have looked closer, and seen how, in the distance, the door to the building my room was in had been forced open. I would have seen the black sheen of the trail bike that had been poorly hidden behind some bushes. I would have felt some kind of charge in the air; I would have known instinctively that something was wrong.

But I wasn't the old, full-eyed me, and I saw and felt none of these things. We came into the sanctuary grounds, covered by that blanking sheet of desire, and only noticed what was happening when it was deliberately revealed to us. As we approached Alec's room someone stepped out from behind one of the ruined enclosures. Thin-limbed, shaking with energy, male. Closer to a boy than a man. A clutch of hair sprang wildly from his head, and dirt, sweat, exhaustion and emotion had muddied his face into an extraordinary contortion. He was trying to keep his expression still, but I could see that he was so angry and scared that he was nearly crying.

We stopped walking. Alec held out both his arms. The boy shook, and raised the northerner's gun.

Time slowed. I stared at this boy. He was familiar to me. I was trying to place him, while trying to stay calm. I didn't want to spook him with any sudden movements. Alec was talking to him, saying hello, that we had no money but lots of food, that he was welcome to have some, that everything was going to be okay. He introduced himself to the boy, then introduced me. When he said my name the boy began shouting, saying he knew who I was, he knew exactly who I was, and that's when my memory clicked. It was the boy from the mountain. The son of the woman's friend.

Recognition must have appeared on my face, unlocking something within him. The arm holding the gun started wobbling, and he began shouting: How does it feel to be followed? How does it feel to be followed? How does it feel to be followed?

He was spitting with each yell. Alec tried to interrupt him, speaking in a calm, soothing tone, but the boy ignored him.

How does it feel to be followed? How does it feel to be followed?

I didn't move. I didn't say anything. Despite his yelling, everything felt quiet. The trees behind the boy were so pale, so dusty blue and faded green. I let out a breath. I remembered how the mountain woman had received a bullet from this gun, and wondered if my body would crumple in the same way hers had. I looked at the boy's shaking arm. I thought of the ocean in my aunt's throat, of the northerner wrapped in salt and blood. A great sense of relief came over me. I stared into the boy's red-cracked eyes, and I waited.

I'm not sure what I would have done differently, even now. I don't know how I could have stopped what happened next, if there's anything I could have said or done. I just wish that, like me, Alec had waited. I wish he'd watched the light on those dusty-blue leaves. I wish he'd stood still, and focused on the stillness of the air, and not taken that sudden step. I wish he hadn't chosen to do that, to move his body between the boy's and mine. Nobody knows what a child with a gun will do. Alec's superiors had been right: he was a terrible soldier.

He moved and the boy, who had forgotten him, flinched, and let his fear and rage and exhaustion and nerves convulse into a squeezing of his finger. The gun fired. I jumped. A ringing took up in my ears. In front of me Alec stumbled, made a choking sound, and gave himself to the gravel at his feet.

HOW MUCH BLOOD runs in a body? Too much, I think. Too much to stay in precious equilibrium, whenever the skin's dam bursts. But when Alec spilled too much of his blood into the gaps of the sanctuary's gravel, I hollowed out before he did. Even as his life rushed out of the hole in his chest, what was left of my own life poured from my mouth, my nose, my ears. I felt it wick away from the moisture on the surface of my eye before he was finished moistening the grey gravel red.

I scrabbled over his torso, mumbling and frantic, pressing at the hole that led to his heart. The boy was staring at us, saying: No, no, no. I balled up the lower hem of Alec's shirt and pressed it to the wound as the boy's words returned to shouts. And when I saw the glassy glint of Alec's eyes and collapsed onto him, shivering and shrieking, the boy also shrieked, before he aimed the gun once more at me, and pulled the trigger again.

No bullet or sound followed. In all the years I'd kept it, I never counted the ammunition in the pistol's clip. I'd convinced myself I'd never use it, and part of this conviction came from refusing to know how many bullets it held. That its original owner had only filled it with two rounds was as surprising to me as it was to the boy. I thought he'd run, but he fell to the ground beside me, staring at Alec's body in rank, formless horror.

We stayed there for a few minutes. Perhaps it was as long as a quarter of an hour. I ignored the boy. I kept my fingers on Alec's neck and cheek until he began to cool. And at the grace of the northerner, my life continued.

I HAVE MADE a lot of mistakes, but I like to think that I haven't repeated many of them. There's a good chance I'm wrong, but it's a thought that keeps me upright, when everything else begins to crowd at me.

When Alec died I scraped a place lower than I'd ever gone before. Lower than seemed possible while still being alive. But somehow, in the sickening, emptying howl of his death, I held on to the lessons of my mistakes. I looked back to a cold beach, an even colder ocean. I remembered bloody waves. I remembered the freshening scent of pine trees, the dark height of a mountain, how a gun felt as it erupted in my fingers. Then I looked again at the boy, and approached him the way one should approach a broken child—with concern, a net of safety, and something like love.

I walked to his side, dropped to a crouch, helped him up. From the expression on his face I could see that he still wanted me to die, even wracked as he was by shame and horror. I started telling him that it was okay, that everything was going to be okay. He didn't say anything, so I told him we should go inside, that we could deal with this—this being Alec's corpse— later on. I said we should sit down, have something to eat and drink, that there was a heater in the kitchen he could use to warm himself up.

He wrenched his arm out of my grip and turned away from Alec's body.

You shot her, he said. She was unarmed and you shot her, and before that you tortured her, and you used my father and me to get to her. She never did anything to you—she never did anything to anyone...

On he went, detailing my crimes on the mountain. If only he knew what else I'd done. It might have spurred him to find a knife and cut my throat. All I could do was let him talk and tire. When finally he stopped I said that he was right, and that I was sorry, and that I wish I hadn't done any of those things, but I had.

These simple admissions confused him. I suppose that, in his head, I was a storybook monster who took delight in causing harm and glee in killing. He looked back at Alec and shuddered. The paleness of the boy's skin was close to alabaster, magnified by the dark locks of his wet hair, the chestnut gleam of his reddened eyes.

And now this happened. If it weren't for you, I wouldn't have—

It's okay. It's not your fault.

The boy didn't pick up on what saying those words cost me.

And you took the bird, he shouted. You gave it to the army! They're probably doing experiments on it. Dad says they'll try and make it rain whenever they want, or grow frost on the farms of people who don't do what they say, or control storms and floods and droughts, and nobody will know how to stop them, and things will get even worse, and—

The bird is in there, I interrupted, pointing at the aviary.

I looked at Alec. There was nothing in him to look back. No quiet words. No touch on my back, light as fog.

We were going to bring it back.

I DON'T THINK the boy believed me. Not about the bird, and not that we were planning to return it. But he consented to come inside and drink some hot milk, shower, rest in a blanketed bed. He took the pistol with him, even though it was empty, carrying it like it held a talismanic power—something I noted with bitter irony.

When he woke up, he found me at the aviary. With the boy asleep, Alec's death had hit me without borders or mercy, and I was a sobbing, mindless mess. I heard the door open, saw the boy approach, empty gun wedged into the slack elastic of his pants, and I tried to stop crying, but I couldn't. All I could do was throw an arm out at the glassed enclosure.

There.

The boy turned. I was wiping at my eye, trying to claw together some composure, when I heard him gasp. As my vision cleared I was able to look up and see him standing close to the glass. On the other side was the rain heron, perched on a branch. It was regarding the boy as it preened at its feathers. The boy stared back, awestruck. It occurred to me that he'd probably never seen it before; that even in the clearing when I'd shot the woman in front of him, the bird had been hidden by the oilcloth; that his belief in it had been an act of faith.

Suddenly the bird spritzed into a cloud of vapour, which floated towards the glass. As it approached the boy leaned in, his nose inches from the glass. Just before it met the barrier, the vapour slowly reformed into the bird, in a watery construction I'd never seen in such detail, and landed on a mound of dirt a metre or two from the edge of the enclosure. It cocked its head and fixed the boy with a curious stare.

He stared back. A scene of wonder and reverence. At last, he spoke.

You were really going to bring it back?

We really were.

Why should I believe you?

I threw my arms back, exposing the ugliness of my grief, although he still wasn't looking at me.

I don't know. I can't make you. But...

I left the word hanging, trying to draw his attention. Eventually he looked over, and saw the red mess of my face.

I'll need help, I said.

WE BURIED ALEC next to Gladstone and Ramiro. There was just enough space for a grave big enough to hold him. I started with the shovel, but the boy soon took it from me, saying that it was his fault we had to dig it, so he'd do the digging. I could have resisted, but it didn't seem worth it.

I watched him toil at the dirt: he an angry adolescent, I an adult who'd made awful mistakes, creating a grave that shouldn't be necessary. When the déjà vu came it was cruel, and it nearly tipped me into the hole, but the boy saved me by describing his journey here.

He'd stolen the trail bike from a neighbour and followed us down the mountain as soon as he could get away from his father. Through the farmland we'd been easy to track, he told me—our truck had left clear trails in the road, and kicked up dust he could follow without getting close enough to reveal himself. The valley of the lake was easy, too. He just had to dodge the reaching holly and follow the highway. It was only when we ascended to the plateau that he'd lost us. At first he'd kept going straight, and found the other soldiers breaking into a fishing resort. But he'd seen that I wasn't with them, so he doubled back. From there he'd spent days crisscrossing the roads and trails, shivering through cold camps, running low on food, finding no sign. He'd thought the road passed straight through the forest of cider gums, so delayed investigating it until he'd covered every other path on the plateau. It was only on the morning of the shooting that he'd plunged into the trees, and wound down the driveway to find the sanctuary. He'd only been there long enough to kick his way through a few buildings and grab the gun he'd found in my room before we returned.

When he finished talking, the hole was rough and uneven but as deep as his neck, and I told him it would do. He climbed out, and together we slung Alec's cold and hardened body into the earth. I took the shovel from the boy and began heaving dirt onto Alec's chest. The boy kicked more of it down. At some point I began crying again, and for a while I forgot that I wanted to help the boy, and how I had decided that I wanted to keep living. I cursed the northerner and his two-bullet limit. The hole filled, and Alec, all of Alec, disappeared.

I DON'T KNOW when the boy decided to help me. It could have been when I told him the bird was still with me, or when he learned of our plan, or as I broke apart at the burial. I suspect it was when he saw the bird with his own eyes.

Not long after we buried Alec, he asked how I was planning to get the bird back in the cage. I told him I wasn't sure. I'd thought of heating the aviary, putting fans through the door, forcing the creature into a cloud I could collect in a bottle. Half-thoughts of vacuums had occurred to me too, as had chemical solutions that I could use to corner and subdue it.

Let me try, the boy said, seeing my hesitation. I think it trusts me.

The bravado of youth. I had no reserves to argue.

I followed as he took the cage into the aviary, closing the door of the building behind me, and waited, hanging back. The boy sat on the floor in front of the door to the enclosure. Soon the bird flashed into being, falling as thick rain into itself, right in front of him, on the other side of the glass. Bubbles rose from its back. Its beak opened, and I heard the sound of a breaking wave. The boy waited. I waited. The bird preened, flapped, and then, just as quickly as it had appeared, it came apart in a spray of hanging mist.

The boy stared. The mist hovered. After a minute he turned to me. I saw his face fold, his confidence fail, and I was reminded of how young he was. He'd thought this would work—that looking into a creature's soul could somehow win its trust. I tried to think of something comforting to say, before an idea occurred to me.

I'd been carrying it for so long, and had never found a

proper use for it. For years I'd thought it would one day come in handy, either as a weapon, a distraction or a bartering tool. But I'd never needed it. I'd only used it once, and that was recently. It hadn't even been necessary—I'd just wanted to cheer Daniel and the men up.

I told the boy to wait, then went to my room to retrieve it. When I returned I was holding it before me in a tight grip. The boy looked suspicious. I waved it at him, trying to smile, but he didn't understand. I supposed there was no reason he would— and that I may as well just try it.

I took a deep breath, looked into the mist, and opened the door to the enclosure. The mist picked up on the change in the air and began wafting towards the aperture, and as it did I unscrewed the lid of the jar I was holding. The ink sloshed, glossy-dark in the glass. For a moment, I remembered taking it from my aunt's house. I remembered opening my skin to draw it from the ocean. I felt a throb in the old scars on my forearm, and then I hurled the glinting liquid into the centre of the approaching cloud.

The ink met the mist in a wild, brilliant confluence. The liquids merged in the air, and began to spit and roil as they raced through a swirl of colours, forming the vague shape of a cloud. Purple-green dominated its hazy body. Orange, vaporous tendrils darted from its edges. Its inner depths held the darkest wink of black, along with flashes of sharp light that could have been miniature forks of lightning. A tiny clap of thunder followed each flash, even as multicoloured rain began to spatter the aviary floor.

I heard the boy gasp, but I didn't take my eyes off the shifting cloud. I waited for it to settle, for it to assume a manageable form, although I didn't know if something like that would actually happen. I realised that I had no idea what would come next, and that this might have been a very bad plan.

After a few minutes the floating storm of colour began to reveal something: the rain heron. It came slowly into view, in the centre of the riotous mist. At first it was just a wing, then a talon. Then a beak showed itself. Eventually the entire bird swam into its own shape, hanging in the flickering colour. Its body was limp, although its eyes were wide and rolling.

I grabbed the cage, its door still closed, and pushed it into the mist, which offered no resistance. Through the cloud the bars went, then through the body of the bird. Its eyes continued to spin, and it didn't notice as it returned to its prison. I wanted to say sorry, to apologise to the creature in a meaningful way. But I did not have the art of apology—I never really have. I just watched the bursts of colour rolling through the bird's wet body, and remembered how squid would hang in the cold ocean, before I tossed the wax-marred cloth over the cage's frame.

The colour disappeared from the room, as quickly as it had sprung to life. I retreated from the enclosure, cage in hand. Everything felt muted, forlorn. Cider-gum leaves showed blue-green through the glass roof. The boy was looking at me as if I had told him a terrible secret, or had revealed a different, truer version of myself—as if I had torn off my skin and shown him my bones.

OUT IN THE air, in the peace and power of the cider-gum forest, I slid the cage onto the back seat of Alec's utility. The boy's trail bike fitted on the tray, and we threw our bags and whatever food we thought might last into the cabin beside the cage. I asked him if he knew how to drive. He hesitated, saying he technically knew how to operate a car, that it couldn't be too different from a bike. I climbed into the driver's seat and told him he'd have to let me know if I was drifting, or taking corners badly, as my eyesight wasn't what it once was.

Over three days we crossed the damp, shining highlands, our time brightened by the persistent beauty of the landscape. We didn't speak much. Each night the boy slept in the utility, with the northerner's empty pistol still looped into his belt. I had my tent. We woke to the call of birds we could not see, the flash of new-fallen snow.

We passed no other vehicles—not in the highlands, not at any time on our trip. After crossing the plateau we descended to the golden prairie, where falcons still dived into the long, feathery grass. Beyond that we dipped into the valley of the lake. The forest was as green and thick as I remembered— tough oak, patched birch, dark-shining holly—and the lake still flat, huge and steely.

Once we'd reached the floor of the valley I found it hard to concentrate on the road. I was so distracted by the lake's reflections, and the dense greenery of the forest, and the cold romance of the hills beyond the water. I kept staring at the rough, tumbling stone fences that stitched the steep fields together and wondering how old they were, how many generations had come and gone since the stones were first stacked together.

Watching the world and thinking about fences helped me forget about Alec, even if only for a few moments. Again and again he returned to me. I saw him walking in the gums, through corridors of lichened rock. I felt him knock against my shoulder. I closed my eye, and saw him dead. When I did that, the utility swerved. Beside me, the boy slept.

In the late afternoon we passed the small collection of houses by the water—the ones the men and I had seen on our way to the sanctuary. Smoke still rose from the chimneys, but this time I decided to stop. The light was fading and we needed to camp somewhere. I no longer cared if someone saw us.

I pitched my tent near the water, and once it was up I walked down the jetty. It was short, almost quaint, built with wide gaps between its handsome wooden slats. The boy came with me, probably wondering what we were doing. I sat down, hung my legs over the edge of the timber.

The sun had fallen behind the hills. Only faint slants of light were left, climbing over the humped, muted-green summits. When the stars began to show, the boy turned to me.

I'm sorry I shot your friend. I didn't mean to.

I breathed deep and slow before I answered.

I know. You were trying to shoot me.

He opened his mouth to defend himself, but I waved him down.

I'm not objecting. I wish he hadn't moved. I wish you had shot me. But here we are.

At that, he said nothing. The stars grew in number and brightness. The forest went dark on the edge of the shining lake.

WE GOT UP early the next morning and were on the road before the sun was fully risen. Through the holly-hedge tunnel we drove, before we climbed the far hill of the valley and emerged onto the long plain of abandoned farms. We passed the stone house where I'd hit Daniel. I stared down the gravel driveway, at the sombre grey building, and remembered how hard I'd struck him, and the look on his face after he'd recovered from the blow. After that I stopped paying much attention to the world outside the windows. The boy stayed quiet, and the bird made no fuss. The only way I could tell it still lived was the occasional huff of steam that fogged at the wax and seeped under the curtain of its cloth. That night we camped in a paddock full of cruel tall thistles.

The next day was much the same. The only real change was that both the boy and I became restless. We knew how close we were to our destination, and we fidgeted in our seats, fiddling with mirrors, seatbelts and sun visors. Soon after we began driving, we passed a place where a river broke into several streams, and that afternoon we were climbing through foothills covered in pines.

The trees thickened around us and my nerves began to rise. My original plan had been to return the bird to its grotto alone, or with Alec. But as it was, travelling with the boy, there seemed no way I'd do it without first going to the village. I wanted to talk this over, to explain my plan to the boy, but he brought it up before I could find the words.

I'll direct you to my dad's house.

He looked back at the cage.

He'll know what to do.

I couldn't fault his logic, and I couldn't argue without revealing my cowardice. So I nodded. Not long after, we crested the final rise and entered the village. My nerves began to shake out as sweat, as trembling fingers, as shallow breaths. I remembered the things I'd ordered my men to do, the last time I'd been in this place. I remembered the boy's father—how he had tried to calm me down after I'd lost my eye, and how I'd kicked out his legs and screamed at him. I remembered the way his face had fractured when I shot his companion. My vision blurred, and the car veered across the road.

Here, said the boy. Stop here.

I heard him late, and braked suddenly. The car lurched to a stop. We were outside a small house built with orange terracotta-like bricks. The street around it was empty. The boy jumped out and, before I could say anything, marched towards the door, which burst open as he was halfway across the road. A man I recognised rushed out, ran to the boy, and took him in a low, fierce embrace. The boy returned the hug, staying as silent as his father. I could see tears blotching the man's face, and his shoulders and back were heaving.

I didn't want to get out of the car, but I knew I had to. I gave them a few moments together before opening my door. By then they'd let each other go and were speaking. I'd hoped the boy had mentioned me, had prepared his father for the shock, but from the way the man's face still glowed with joy and relief I could see that my presence was yet to be raised. There was nothing to be done. I stepped onto the road, closed the door, and waited to be noticed.

When the boy's father saw me his face blanched, and he

grabbed at his son and pulled him behind his own body. It reminded me of Alec, stepping into the path of a bullet meant for me, and the arrival of that memory, along with the nerves and shame I was already feeling, nearly pitched me to my knees. But I stayed upright. I held out my hands, showing empty palms. The man shuffled back. His face had lost its love, its joy, and was drawn up tight and cold with fear. The boy was saying that it was okay, that I wasn't going to hurt anyone. His father wasn't listening.

I didn't think talking would help. There was nothing I could say to this man that would make him change his mind about me. There was no way I could make things right, other than by what I had come there to do. I reached into the truck and grabbed the cage. I placed it on the road and stepped back.

The boy had wriggled free. Finally the man looked down at him. He saw the gun in his son's waistband, and flinched. He looked back at me, at the empty holster at my hip. Wariness began to swim across his face, taking over from the terror.

I took a step forward. I pointed at the cage, and was about to tell him everything when a sound intruded.

A click, then a creak. The door that the boy's father had come through was reopening. I waited for another son, or a daughter, or his wife to come out with a shotgun, ready to blast me to pieces. If that had happened, I don't think I would have run.

The door opened. It was a woman, and she was unarmed. She was strikingly thin, and she wore a thick woollen cap on her head, a scarf twisted around her neck and shoulders. She must have been the boy's mother, but she did not run to him the way his father had, which I thought strange. She came through the doorway in a slow shuffle, and stopped to lean against the outside of the house, as if that short trip had weakened her.

I glanced back at the father, hoping he was beginning to calm. But he was looking at the woman at the door, and seemed worried. The boy was looking at her, too, with the same apprehensiveness. Puzzled, I returned my gaze to the woman. With a stiff twist of her neck she looked at me, and I could tell that the movement cost her something more than physical discomfort. And then, finally, I saw her.

It was the eyes; I found her in her eyes. They settled on me, and I saw them as they were when her head had been lying on my lap, after I had wrecked her world and pushed her to breaking. I did not need her to do what she did next to recognise her—which I'm sure she knew, but she did it anyway. With slow hands she unwound the scarf, revealing the purpled birth of a huge, X-shaped scar, mottled and warped into the base of her throat. Blue threads poked out all over the shape of it, the ends of amateur stitches, running haywire through her skin.

I find it hard to describe how I felt then, or what I was thinking. Everything was still. I was hit by shock, and relief, and a deep, flesh-rattling dread. My mouth went dry. I gazed at the boy, demanding with my eye to know why he hadn't told me she had survived. He shrugged, but not kindly or apologetically, communicating that it was a reprieve I hadn't deserved. I looked back at the mountain woman, who was staring at me, her eyes hard as ever, the blue threads snaking through her flesh where my bullet should have killed her. I opened my mouth. I came very close to climbing back in the utility. But in the end

252

I did the only thing that could distract us all from the torture of this reunion. I reached down, grabbed the cage and lifted it into the air.

We all stood still. I wanted desperately to say something, to tell the woman I was sorry, to tell her what had happened to me. Seeing her alive, I suddenly wanted her to understand me, to know me. But even as I struggled for words, I saw that she was no longer looking in my direction. She was staring at the cage.

Wet, soft light had begun to blink through the wax.

THE BOY SPOKE first. As the heron's light played, he began telling his father and the woman I'd shot about what had happened on the plateau. He told them that I was there to return the bird, that I knew I'd made a mistake. He repeated that I wasn't going to hurt anyone. I stayed silent and kept holding the cage.

When he stopped speaking, his father looked at me, fear still on his face, but a question, also. I realised he was asking me if what his son said was true. I nodded, and tried to look trustworthy. The man let out a slow breath, then turned away from me. Without speaking to the boy he ushered him inside the house, deftly pulling the pistol from the boy's belt at the same time. The mountain woman went with them. Still I stood there, unmoving, until she turned on the threshold, regarded me for another moment, then indicated the house with a stiff nod.

It wasn't easy to follow her. Again I came close to climbing into the utility and driving away. But somehow I gathered the courage to go in that little house, where I found the three of them sitting at a small table. I put the cage by the door and lowered myself into a chair. The boy was still talking, telling his father about his trip across the plains, about all the things he'd seen. He didn't mention Alec, or what had happened at the sanctuary.

I didn't speak and I avoided looking at the mountain woman as she stared straight at me. I still wanted her to know me, and I felt a great need to apologise, but every time I opened my mouth I realised how absurd that would be.

Eventually she put me out of my misery by pulling a pen and pad from her pocket and scribbling. She ripped the paper from its spiral spine and held it out to me.

My name is Ren.

I read it, then looked up. The mountain woman kept staring at me, her face grim, and I realised this was important to her, that I know her name.

Oh, I said.

I began introducing myself, then remembered I'd done that before, weeks earlier, by her cave. I trailed off. When I looked at her again she motioned at the mess of rent flesh and twine in her neck, then pointed at her closed mouth. She scribbled another note.

I never talked much anyway.

I opened my mouth, but no words came out. I looked at Ren's scar and suddenly saw Alec, the blood rushing from his chest. Again I tried to speak, and managed only a high, fractured wheeze.

But I could see she was smiling—that for her there was a glint of dark humour in the fact that we were meeting again, like this. Her smile cracked something open in me. I was shaking. I think I started to hyperventilate. She gave a wave of her hand, wrote another note, and passed it to me.

Did you really come here to return it?

I slowed my breathing and met her gaze.

Yes, I said. I really did.

She smiled again, sad and pained, before putting her pen back to her notepad.

At least you're seeing clearer.

In all those times I'd closed my eye and seen her, it had never occurred to me that she might be funny.

THAT EVENING REN and I walked into the pines beyond the edge of town. The boy and his father stayed behind.

She led the way and I carried the cage. It felt wrong to keep the heron imprisoned like that in her presence, but Ren didn't object. She just walked to the trees, and at the edge of the forest turned to see if I was following her. She saw me hesitating, beckoned with her hand. Then she threaded into the tree line.

The pines were as thick as I remembered, the air still dense with their smell. Dried needles slid under my boots. Other trees I couldn't name were scattered among them, along with mossy logs, boulders, and hundreds of kinds of bracken, bush and sprout. Heavy ravens flapped through the lower parts of the canopy, trailing low, dry calls. Other birds chirped and whistled, but I did not see them. Creeks sang with damp rhythm.

The sounds and scenery, the smells—the freshening pine, the earthy rot of fallen wood—all of it combined to remind me of how relaxed I'd felt in this place, and of what I'd done here, amid all the calm beauty. I looked ahead at Ren. Her pace was slow, and she had to stop every ten or fifteen minutes to catch her breath. Yet her movements were confident, purposeful, and she never slipped or stumbled on the roots and rocks of the forest floor.

The sun lowered, its fading light broken by the forest roof. On we went, apparently to where I'd captured the bird. It seemed impossible we'd venture that high, especially given Ren's condition. But I looked at her again, at her steady, implacable stride, and I began to wonder if we were climbing all the way up the peak, to the grotto at its heart.

We reached a wide stream, and Ren stopped. I thought she

was resting, but when I felt her eyes settle on me I realised we were doing more than that. I lowered the cage to the ground.

Here?

She nodded. I was going to ask why, but she turned to look upstream. I followed her gaze and saw that the water ran in an uncommonly straight course. Pines lined its banks, all the way to the rocky heights. The stream eventually disappeared into a cliff, which ran right up to a high, weathered peak, framed by the night sky.

I turned back to Ren. She indicated the cage. No light showed through the wax.

I hesitated.

You should do it, I said.

Ren looked back at the peak, her neck cocked. She crossed her arms. Still I did not move. I didn't want to be the one to release the bird. I didn't feel like I deserved it. Finally, she ended our stalemate by scribbling one of her notes.

You're the one who took it.

By the time I'd digested her words she'd hoisted herself onto a large rock and leaned back on her arms, an expectant expression on her face. I turned to the cage. I looked back at her. My thoughts wobbled, my neck felt hot, and before I let myself think about it any further I ripped the oilcloth free and staggered a few steps backwards.

Within the bars sat the rain heron. It was in its most animal form—a normal, if watery and ghostly, heron. The only difference to its appearance was the splash of colour in its wings—the blend of red and green, yellow and violet that had come from its amalgamation with the ink.

257

It appeared to be sleeping, but seconds after I removed the cloth it stirred. Perhaps it was the sound of the stream, or the brightness of the moon. The bird opened its shimmering eyes and stood. It stretched its neck. It regarded the forest, the running water, the distant peak. It looked up at the sky. It looked at Ren, then at me. I suddenly felt sure that it would rush to me in a storm of colour and take my remaining eye: that I would finally receive the blindness my actions had earned.

But the bird just picked its way past the bars, carefully sliding its body through the metal. The rainbow on its wings caught on the iron, sluicing out of the feathers like stripped oil. When it had emerged completely from the cage it was once again a pale, pure blue. All that remained of its temporary colouring ran as thick, shining ink down the cage's bars.

I did not move. The bird looked again at the peak, then gave its wings a tremendous flap. Cold water sprayed my face. The rain heron rose into the air, high and fast, to hover briefly above the stream before plunging down into it in a steep dive. A wave broke from the place it entered the water, and began travelling upstream, against the current. I watched it grow in size and gather pace as it moved, an impossible wave that hastened up the wild water until it was gone from view.

ON THE WAY back to the village I finally apologised. With the bird released my thoughts had cleared, and I found I could say the things that been tumbling in my mind ever since I'd discovered Ren had survived my bullet.

I told her I was sorry for what I'd done to her, and for what I'd done to her friends. I said that I had been wrong, and cruel, and that I didn't expect her to forgive me. I didn't offer any explanations, didn't give an excuse, lay any blame, or try to convince her that my actions had been a kind of calculated mercy. I didn't tell her about my life, the things I'd experienced. I just apologised. It didn't make me feel any better, but I felt glad that I'd said it.

She was still walking ahead of me, so I had no way of knowing what she thought of my words. But a few minutes after I gave her my apology, she stopped. We had come to a grassy glade. A gap in the trees let in the shine of the moon and stars. She turned and studied me, her expression as blank and unimpressed as ever. I looked around, trying to see if there was a significance to this place. When I looked back at her, she was scribbling yet another note.

It was almost too dark to read, even in the unbroken moonlight. I peered closely until I could make out the words.

Are you going to stay?

Something churned within my stomach, my chest. It had never occurred to me. I stared at her, confused.

Do you think I should?

She seemed to think about it, before shaking her head. Another note followed.

Probably not a good idea.

I nodded. I made to start walking again, but Ren hadn't moved. She still had that thoughtful look. I waited, and as I did a question occurred to me—one I'd thought of often during our first encounter, in that time that felt so long ago, but had never asked.

Why did you come here?

Her face lost its look of contemplation. She waited a moment, taking in the moon, the trees, then me, before writing a note.

I had a son.

She frowned, and wrote another one.

Have a son.

I tried to make my face look sympathetic.

The coup?

She nodded. Her pen scratched again.

Maybe one day he'll find me here.

Then she smiled. We resumed walking. Clouds covered the stars: I couldn't see where we were going. But Ren did not hesitate in her path, and I had her steady back to follow. It made me feel safe, even as my feet fumbled in the darkness.

THAT NIGHT I slept in the utility. In the early morning I woke to someone knocking on the window. It was the boy. He invited me in for breakfast, and I had no way of refusing.

Inside, there was toast and porridge. Ren ate slowly, in tiny mouthfuls, wincing each time she swallowed. Small trails of tears crept down her cheeks, though her face stayed still. I felt sick, and tried to look away. It was only porridge, but it was as if she were eating glass. I ate as fast as I could, thanked the boy's father, and went back outside.

The sun was only half-risen, but the day already felt hot. The pines loomed, weighed heavy with needles and cones. I heard the door open, heard footsteps approaching.

The boy's father walked forward. I realised I still didn't know his name. He tried to hand me the northerner's pistol; I refused. He put it back in his pocket and nodded, a motion of acknowledgment, though I didn't know what he was acknowledging. An understanding, perhaps. The most I could ask for.

Ren and the boy had come out, too. He was dawdling near the doorway, but she was pulling on a large backpack and adjusting the wide brim of a hat. Without looking at me or the boy's father she began walking towards the same gap in the trees that we'd taken the night before. When she reached it, she turned and waited.

I looked at her, unsure of what was happening, until the boy's father began to speak.

She's going back up the mountain. Only for a few hours. There are some things she left in her cave, and she wants to check on what's left of her garden. Set some traps.

I nodded. Ren kept waiting.

She was wondering, the boy's father continued, if you'd like to go with her. Just for the day.

I looked at her again. I thought about our trip the previous evening. The trees, the streams, the sounds and smell and stillness of it all. I thought of low-flapping ravens, of the greenness of moss. I thought of how good it would be to tread through that world, to do it not just today but again and again, following Ren's back, sliding into all that quiet, dappled beauty.

And then I thought of the breakfast we'd just shared. Of the agony in her gulps, the tears on her cheeks. Of her still-healing wound, the scar it would leave—of her silence.

I shook my head, but did not trust myself to speak.

The man turned back to the house, where his son hovered beneath the eave. The boy waved at me. I waved back as, moving automatically, I pulled open the door of the utility.

I looked one last time at Ren. She adjusted her pack, then gave a small nod. I felt suddenly transparent, as if she could see through my skin and flesh, and into the air behind me.

Then she turned and began to trudge forward, slow and sure, into the trees. When she was out of sight I climbed into the driver's seat, started the engine and drove away.

I LEFT THE mountain, and Ren left my darkness. I no longer saw her when I closed my eyelid. Instead, I saw what most people see: strange shapes, points of light, nothing. But while my dreams settled, I did not. I could not stay still. And while I saw many pleasant places, they were joined by just as many broken ones.

I went looking for something like solace. I didn't find it, no matter where I went, which ended up being just about everywhere. Always I expected the military to find me, but they never did. I supposed the generals were too busy clinging to power to bother with a crippled deserter. The odd patrol, the occasional cold remnants of a burnt town showed that things weren't going well, for the military or for the people they ruled. But I didn't stop to find out. It never seemed worth the time.

I rumbled over the farmlands, skirted the cities, looking for somewhere to collect myself. But everywhere I stopped my skin jangled, and every place felt unsteady beneath my feet. The days of travel turned into weeks. My skills and strength made me useful to the various communities I passed through, so I was always able to feed myself and organise shelter. But I had done so much in the coup that might be remembered, and I didn't trust that I wouldn't run into someone with memories of my actions.

Most nights I fell asleep thinking of the rain heron on the mountain, diving in and out of its high pool with only moss and stars for company.

Eventually I came, by way of the old, perilous hill road, back to my home town in the south. I arrived in spring, a time I remembered as chilly and bright-skied. As I neared the port

I began to skirt the granite hills of my youth, although their smooth domes were capped by snow—lingering signs of a winter that must have been even harsher than the one I remembered so well. These snowy peaks reflected the southern sun in a different, sharper way from the crystal of the granite. I tried to avoid looking at it, but the light lanced at my vision for the brief last stage of my drive.

In town, I found that people had returned, although none that I recognised. They had boats, and they worked at the dock, but I learned that none of them were going after squid. They were trawling for fish. Any fish—they didn't care what kind. They told me that almost all of their catch was ground up into fertiliser. When I asked about ink, trying to figure out if any of them knew how to harvest it, they laughed at me, as if I was bringing up a fairy tale. I thought of showing them the sea–sky painting in the pub, but the pub was no longer there. It had burned down, and only a few beams of charred, frozen wood remained.

I walked on, looking at the buildings that had once been my school, my friends' houses, avoiding the street that held my aunt's cottage. I shuffled down the long white beach that ran away from the township until I felt something small break apart inside me, and I turned back. That night I slept in the hills, shivering in my tent under every blanket and piece of clothing I owned. In the morning I looked back at the town—at the whitening waves, the whiter sand, the mean collection of fishing boats. I left, and did not return.

By then it was the third year after I had returned the bird. That summer millions of fish rose to the surface of the country's largest river, bloating the banks with rot. Dry lightning licked once-wet forests into infernos. Peat fires burned underground in the marshes of the highlands, fires that might not go out for centuries. A few months later, frost entombed the roots of palm trees on the coasts. So much was ruined, either slowly or in red instants, and nothing was getting better, and nobody was doing enough about it. And through the quiet carnage of the world, I kept moving.

SOMETIMES I STILL feel that phantom chill—the sensation of air on the back of my lost eye. At first it didn't worry me. I took it as a sign of my connection to the creature that had taken it from me, and that if I was feeling it, the bird must be healthy and free. But as years passed it began happening more and more, in all sorts of places, at random times. In the lush garden of a former city park, as I harvested pumpkins for semi-militant horticulturalists; under a hot lowland sun, as I taught survivalists how to gut rabbits; on the stony shore of a lake at dusk, as I angled for oily-fleshed salmon. At all these times and more I would feel it: the cold night grazing at my old, long-gone eye.

The more it happened, the more it reminded me of how I had lost it, of the things I'd done, of the person I had been and perhaps always would be. I knew it was a phantom pain, but that made the feeling of it no less real. It came to be unbearable, this fake scratch of breeze and its associated memories, and I decided to do something about it.

I was staying in a small town that had been mostly unaf-fected by the coup and what had followed. I cast around for a psychologist, but nobody had ever met one. I would have settled for a doctor to talk it over with, but the town's last GP had been hauled into the army and never returned. There was a retired nurse, but he drank whisky for breakfast, and I didn't want him to know anything about me.

I considered my options. I couldn't remember if there were riots happening, if people generally thought we were now lurching in a good direction or a bad one. Certainly the weather was still worsening. Either way, I didn't want to have to go into a city, where the doctors would be. The thought of crowds made me flinch. But I had reached a point where the wind passing over my missing eye was jerking me awake three, four, five, times a night. I didn't like my chances of finding any mindfulness experts or alternative therapists—everyone who the military had thought even vaguely resembled a hippie had been killed or chased over the borders during the coup. A lot of that chasing, I remembered, was done by me.

Medical help of some kind was the only option I could come up with. I thought about the part of the country I was in, the places I was near. I imagined a map with the town at the centre of it. My mind roamed over the country surrounding it, the places people lived and didn't, the farms and forests and lakes and hills—I was nowhere near the ocean; I had grown allergic to salted air and the sound of waves—and it dawned on me that help might not be far away.

It didn't take me long to reach the valley. I was sure it was the place. One of the things that had made me such a good soldier was my memory, my attention to detail. I had rarely forgotten the particulars of my orders, my missions, or the soldiers under my command.

Bare orchards greeted me as my car dipped down the valley's green hills, and stone-fruit trees hustled the narrow road. I didn't know where I was going, exactly, but smoke was rising from most of the farmhouses as I descended into the valley's lower corners. After knocking on doors and asking a few questions, I was armed with an address and directions.

I drove for another hour, over stone bridges, around tight bends hemmed by yellow-flowered hedges, and finally across flat fields, trim and ordered. I turned into the driveway I'd been directed to and followed its lines to a red-brick house with a neat lawn. I parked carefully, making sure my tyres didn't damage the grass. I wondered if he was home, and what he'd do when he saw me.

I didn't have to wait. He came out as soon as my foot hit his lawn. I heard warm sounds of people from inside the house, but he closed the door. He had grown a beard, thick and curled, which hid whether or not his features remained youthful. But the rest of him was the same. Still hesitant, cautious. Still coming towards me, a look of concern in his eyes that I remembered so well.

When my medic recognised me he paused, halfway across the lawn. I didn't know how to greet him, so I raised a hand.

Daniel stayed still, glued to that beautiful grass, and I wondered if he was afraid, if he thought I was there to do something terrible. He kept looking, then his eyes and cheeks softened. He must have seen something I wasn't aware of. I thought I looked normal, or as normal as I could in those days. But he was coming to me faster, his strides urgent.

I tried to tell him I wouldn't stay long, that I just wanted some help with my old injury, that I was sorry to leap out of his past like this, but then he was before me, and he was not stopping.

He crashed into me, and I was buffeted by a forceful hug. Half my breath was knocked out of me, and the sudden physical contact jittered my pulse. I found that I was returning his embrace. We stayed there, pressed tight, unmoving.

Something had happened to my throat. My breaths were

coming out shallow and wrong. His beard scratched my ear, which was hot. So, I realised, was my face. I couldn't hold my thoughts straight. My phantom eye flinched from a far-off breeze, but I barely noticed.

ACKNOWLEDGMENTS

Thank you to everyone at Text Publishing, especially my editor, David Winter. Thanks also to James Roxburgh, Emily Bell, Ben Walter, Scott Arnott, and the great love of my life, Emily Bill.

ABOUT THE AUTHOR

Robbie Arnott was a 2019 *Sydney Morning Herald* Best Young Novelist and won the Margaret Scott Prize in the 2019 Tasmanian Premier's Literary Prizes. His widely acclaimed debut, *Flames* (2018), was longlisted for the Miles Franklin Literary Award and shortlisted for, among others, a Victorian Premier's Literary Award and the *Guardian*'s Not the Booker Prize. He lives in Hobart, Tasmania.